HELEN WITH
THE HIGH HAND

ARNOLD BENNETT

HELEN WITH
THE HIGH HAND

ALAN SUTTON
1983

Alan Sutton Publishing Limited
17a Brunswick Road
Gloucester GL1 1HG

First published 1910

Copyright © in this edition 1983
Alan Sutton Publishing Limited

British Library Cataloguing in Publication Data

Bennett, Arnold
   Helen with the high hand
   I. Title
   823'.8[F]   PR6003.E6

   ISBN 0-86299-076-9

Cover picture: detail from The Unconscious Rivals
by Sir Lawrence Alma-Tadema.
City of Bristol Museum and Art Gallery

Typesetting and origination by
Alan Sutton Publishing Limited.
Photoset Bembo 9/10
Printed in Great Britain
by The Guernsey Press Company Limited,
Guernsey, Channel Islands,

BIOGRAPHICAL NOTE

ARNOLD BENNETT (1867–1931) was a successful, prolific and versatile writer, now best known as a novelist whose major works introduced the mainstream of European realism to early twentieth-century English literature. He presented the seamy side of provincial life, dispassionately recording its ugly and sordid features, sometimes ironically and always without censure, in a series of over thirty novels and collections of short stories. Yet he was the author of more than seventy books in all, a cosmopolitan and industrious journalist who performed at many levels of seriousness, a perceptive critic of contemporary music, literature and art, as well as a playwright and essayist who became a popular figure in the early twentieth-century literary establishment.

(Enoch) Arnold Bennett was born on May 27, 1867 at Hanley, Staffordshire, one of the 'Five Towns' (properly six) of the Potteries now comprising Stoke-on-Trent. The eldest of six children of a self-made Methodist provincial solicitor (who had also been a schoolmaster), he was brought up in an atmosphere of sturdy middle-class respectability and self-improvement of an uncommonly cultured and bookish household. He was educated at the Burslem Endowed School and the Middle School at Newcastle-under-Lyme, later attending a local art school (he painted charming watercolours to the end of his life). At the age of 18 he worked as a clerk in his father's office, where he contributed precocious weekly articles to a local newspaper.

He left the Potteries in 1888 for London where, after a period articled to a firm of solicitors, he soon put aside his law studies and laboured to establish himself in journalism. He wrote popular and sensational serial fiction, becoming assistant editor (1893), and later editor (1896–1900), of a women's magazine, *Woman,* where he wrote on a variety of topics from society gossip, fashion and recipés to book and, above all, theatre reviews. His writing was increasingly in demand from other magazines, including the leading critical journal *Academy,* and the popular press. Encouraged by the publication of a short story in the fashionable *Yellow Book* in July 1895, he embarked on a first novel, which was published in 1898 as *A Man from the North* under the influence of John Buchan.

In 1900 he resigned his editorship of *Woman* to become a professional writer, continuing to contribute free-lance short stories and serial novels to magazines. *The Grand Babylon Hotel* (1902), a sensational and popular work in the manner of Ouida, was published in the same year as *Anna of the Five Towns* (1902), a work of serious literary pretensions under the influence of George Moore and Emile Zola. This is now considered one of his best novels, describing against the fictional background of the Five Towns of the Staffordshire Potteries a heroine of honesty and compassion who refuses to compromise with provincial Methodist society.

In 1903, after his father's death, he moved from a farmhouse in the Bedfordshire countryside to metropolitan Paris, in the footsteps of the artists and writers whom he most admired. In Paris he conceived his greatest and best known novel, *The Old Wives' Tale* (1908), which established, and has since largely maintained, his reputation. This is a novel of finely drawn characters set against a vividly realized background: the heroines are two sisters, allegedly inspired by two ungainly elderly women whom he had seen in a Paris restaurant in 1903. When the *Clayhanger* trilogy appeared (1910–1915; reprinted 1925 as *The Clayhanger Family*), his stature as one of the leading serious novelists of the day was confirmed. Showing him as a meticulous and often comic dramatist and historian of life in the Five Towns, it concerns the gloomy life of Edwin Clayhanger and his desperate love for Hilda Lessways and, in the final volume, their life together.

In Paris, Bennett wrested free of his provincial attitudes, becoming a cosmopolitan inhabitant of the Paris of the end of the *belle époque,* a melting-pot of artistic and literary influences and experiment. An early admirer of the French masters, who had been among the first English novelists to learn from studying the technique of Balzac, Flaubert, the de Goncourts, de Maupassant and Zola, his criticism is of a high order; it demonstrates his early appreciation of the contemporary arts, of the Post-impressionist painters, of the ballet of Diaghelev and Stravinsky, as well as of the young writers, including Joyce, D.H. Lawrence and Faulkner. In 1907 he married a French actress, Marguerite Soulie, from whom he was separated in 1921.

When, after ten years in Paris, Bennett returned to England, he was a figure of the literary establishment, rich beyond the dreams of most authors, and offered a knighthood (in 1918; which he declined). He divided his time between London, Paris, a yacht and a country house in Essex, never returning to the Potteries except for brief visits, although they were to continue to provide the imaginative background to his novels. He wrote with remarkable facility, conducting a lecture-tour in the United States of America and publishing novels and short stories, journalism (particularly as a powerful propagandist during the War years, and before them in A.R. Orage's brilliant journal, *New Age*) and a number of plays. The latter include *Milestones* (1912; with E. Knoblock) and *The Great Adventure* (1913; adapted from an earlier novel), which were popular successes.

A precursor of modernism who owed much to the example of the European realists, his reputation suffered a decline after the great novels of the pre-war years: the modernists condemned his technique as providing mere 'photography', for its excessively scientific and unstructured accumulation of details. From this it was retrieved by the publication in 1923 of *Riceyman's Steps,* the last of his major novels and a popular and critical success. It is a brilliant achievement in technique and design, set in the dark and squalid suburbs of London . . . The sinister tale concerns a miserly second-hand book-dealer who starves himself to death and whose contagious passion for thrift dominates his household, with terrible consequences for his wife. Here Bennett's handling of atmosphere, his psychological observation and kindly tolerance of feeling contribute to a final masterpiece.

The Journals of Arnold Bennett 1896–1928, a fascinating

account of his life and times, were edited by Newman Flower (3 vols., 1932–3) after his death of typhoid fever in Marylebone, London, on March 27, 1931.

NICHOLAS MANDER

CHAPTER I

BEGINNING OF THE IDYLL

In the Five Towns human nature is reported to be so hard that
you can break stones on it. Yet sometimes it softens, and then
we have one of our rare idylls of which we are very proud,
while pretending not to be. The soft and delicate South would
possibly not esteem highly our idylls, idyllic for us, and
reminding us, by certain symptoms, that though we never cry
there is concealed somewhere within our bodies a fount of
happy tears.

The town park is an idyll in the otherwise prosaic municipal
history of the Borough of Bursley, which previously had
never got nearer to romance than a Turkish bath. It was once
waste ground covered with horrible rubbish-heaps, and made
dangerous by the imperfectly-protected shafts of disused
coal-pits. Now you enter it by emblazoned gates; it is
surrounded by elegant railings; fountains and cascades babble
in it; wild-fowl from far countries roost in it, on trees with
long names; tea is served in it; brass bands make music on its
terraces, and on its highest terrace town councillors play
bowls on billiard-table greens while casting proud glances on
the houses of thirty thousand people spread out under the
sweet influence of the gold angel that tops the Town Hall
spire. The other four towns are apt to ridicule that gold angel,
which for exactly fifty years has guarded the borough and
only been re-gilded twice. But ask the plumber who last had
the fearsome job of regilding it whether it is a gold angel to be
despised, and – you will see!

The other four towns are also apt to point to their own
parks when Bursley mentions its park (especially Turnhill,
smallest and most conceited of the Five); but let them show a
park whose natural situation equals that of Bursley's park.
You may tell me that the terra-cotta constructions within it

carry ugliness beyond a joke; you may tell me that in spite of the park's vaunted situation nothing can be seen from it save the chimneys and kilns of earthenware manufactories, the scaffoldings of pitheads, the ample dome of the rate-collector's offices, the railway, minarets of nonconformity, sundry undulating square miles of monotonous house-roofs, the long scarves of black smoke which add such interest to the sky of the Five Towns – and, of course, the gold angel. But I tell you that before the days of the park, lovers had no place to walk in but the cemetery; not the ancient churchyard of St. Luke's (the rector would like to catch them at it!) – the borough cemetery! One generation was forced to make love over the tombs of another – and such tombs! – before the days of the park. That is the sufficient answer to any criticism of the park.

The highest terrace of the park is a splendid expanse of gravel, ornamented with flower-beds. At one end is the north bowling-green; at the other is the south bowling-green; in the middle is a terra-cotta and glass shelter; and at intervals, against the terra-cotta balustrade, are arranged rustic seats from which the aged, the enamoured, and the sedentary can enjoy the gold angel.

Between the southernmost seat and the south bowling-green, on that Saturday afternoon, stood Mr. James Ollerenshaw. He was watching a man who earned four-and-six pence a day by gently toying from time to time with a roller on the polished surface of the green. Mr. James Ollerenshaw's age was sixty; but he looked as if he did not care. His appearance was shabby; but he did not seem to mind. He carried his hands in the peculiar horizontal pockets of his trousers, and stuck out his figure, in a way to indicate that he gave permission to all to think of him exactly what they pleased. Those pockets were characteristic of the whole costume; their very name is unfamiliar to the twentieth century. They divide the garment by a fissure whose sides are kept together by many buttons, and a defection on the part of even a few buttons is apt to be inconvenient. James Ollerenshaw was one of the last persons in Bursley to defy fashion in the matter of pockets. His suit was of a strange hot colour – like a brick which, having become very dirty, has been imperfectly cleaned and then powered with sand – made in a hard, eternal, resistless cloth, after a pattern which has not survived the apprenticeship of Five Towns' tailors in London. Scarcely anywhere save on the person of James Ollerenshaw would you see nowadays that cloth, that tint, those very short coat-tails, that curved opening of the waistcoat, or those trouser-pockets. The paper turned-down collar, and the black necktie (of which only one square inch was ever visible), and the paper cuffs, which finished the tailor-made portion of Mr. Ollerenshaw, still linger in sporadic profusion. His low, flat-topped hat was faintly green, as though a delicate fungoid growth were just budding on its black. His small feet were cloistered in small, thick boots of glittering brilliance. The colour of his face matched that of his suit. He had no moustache and no whiskers, but a small, stiff grey beard was rooted somewhere under his chin. He had kept a good deal of his hair. He was an undersized man, with short arms and legs, and all his features – mouth, nose, ears, blue eyes – were small and sharp; his head, as an entirety, was small. His thin mouth was always tightly shut, except when he spoke. The general expression of his face was one of suppressed, sarcastic amusement.

He was always referred to as Jimmy Ollerenshaw, and he may strike you as what is known as a 'character', an oddity. His sudden appearance at a Royal Levée would assuredly have excited remark, and even in Bursley he diverged from the ordinary; nevertheless, I must expressly warn you against imagining Mr. Ollerenshaw as an oddity. It is the most difficult thing in the world for a man named James not to be referred to as Jimmy. The temptation to the public is almost irresistible. Let him have but a wart on his nose, and they will regard it as sufficient excuse for yielding. I do not think that Mr. Ollerenshaw was consciously set down as an oddity in his native town. Certainly he did not so set down himself. Certainly he was incapable of freakishness. By the town he was respected. His views on cottage property, the state of trade, and the finances of the borough were listened to with a respectful absence of comment. He was one of the few who had made cottage property pay. It was said he owned a mile of cottages in Bursley and Turnhill. It was said that, after Ephraim Tellwright, he was the richest man in Bursley. There

was a slight resemblance of type between Ollerenshaw and
Tellwright. But Tellwright had buried two wives, whereas
Ollerenshaw had never got within arm's length of a woman.
The town much preferred Ollerenshaw.

After having duly surveyed the majestic activities of the
ground-man on the bowling-green, and having glanced at his
watch, Mr. Ollerenshaw sat down on the nearest bench; he
was waiting for an opponent, the captain of the bowling-club.
It is exactly at the instant of his downsitting that the drama
about to be unfolded properly begins. Strolling along from the
northern extremity of the terrace to the southern was a young
woman. This young woman, as could be judged from her free
and independent carriage, was such a creature as, having once
resolved to do a thing, is not to be deterred from doing it by
the caprices of other people. She had resolved – a resolution of
no importance whatever – to seat herself on precisely the
southernmost bench of the terrace. There was not, indeed, any
particular reason why she should have chosen the
southernmost bench; but she had chosen it. She had chosen it,
afar off, while it was yet empty and Mr. Ollerenshaw was on
his feet. When Mr. Ollerenshaw dropped into a corner of it
the girl's first instinctive volition was to stop, earlier than she
had intended, at one of the other seats.

Despite statements to the contrary, man is so little like a
sheep that when he has a choice of benches in a park he will
always select an empty one. The rule is universal in England
and Scotland, though elsewhere exceptions to it have been
known to occur. But the girl, being a girl, and being a girl
who earned her own living, and being a girl who brought all
conventions to the bar of her reason and forced them to stand
trial there, said to herself, proudly and coldly: 'It would be
absurd on my part to change my mind. I meant to occupy that
bench, and why should I not? There is amply sufficient space
for the man and me too. He has taken one corner, and I will
take the other. These notions that girls have are silly.' She
meant the notion that she herself had had.

So she floated forward, charmingly and inexorably. She was
what in the Five Towns is called 'a stylish piece of goods.' She
wore a black-and-white frock, of a small check pattern, with a
black belt and long black gloves, and she held over her

serenity a black parasol richly flounced with black lace – a toilet unusual in the district, and as effective as it was unusual. She knew how to carry it. She was a tall girl, and generously formed, with a complexion between fair and dark; her age, perhaps, about twenty-five. She had the eye of an empress – and not an empress-consort either, nor an empress who trembles in secret at the rumour of cabals and intrigues. Yes, considered as a decoration of the terrace, she was possibly the finest, most dazzling thing that Bursley could have produced, and Bursley doubtless regretted that it could only claim her as a daughter by adoption.

Approaching, step by dainty and precise step, the seat invested by Mr. James Ollerenshaw, she arrived at the point whence she could distinguish the features of her forestaller; she was somewhat short-sighted. She gave no outward sign of fear, irresolution, cowardice. But if she had not been more afraid of her own contempt than of anything else in the world, she would have run away; she would have ceased being an empress and declined suddenly into a scared child. However, her fear of her own contempt kept her spine straight, her face towards the danger, and her feet steadily moving.

'It's not my fault,' she said to herself. 'I meant to occupy that bench and occupy it I will. What have I to be ashamed of?'

And she did occupy that bench. She contrived to occupy it without seeing Mr. Ollerenshaw. Each separate movement of hers denied absolutely the existence of Mr. Ollerenshaw. She arranged her dress, and her parasol, and her arms, and the exact angle of her chin; and there gradually fell upon her that stillness which falls upon the figure of a woman when she has definitively adopted an attitude in the public eye. She was gazing at the gold angel, a mile off, which flashed in the sun. But what a deceptive stillness was that stillness! A hammer was hammering away under her breast, with what seemed to her a reverberating sound. Strange that that hammering did not excite attention throughout the park! Then she has the misfortune to think of the act of blushing. She violently willed not to blush. But her blood was too much for her. It displayed itself in the most sanguinary manner first in the centre of each cheek, and it increased its area of conquest until the whole of her visible skin – even the back of her neck and her lobes – had

rosily yielded. And she was one of your girls who never blush!
The ignominy of it! To blush because she found herself within
thirty inches of a man, an old man, with whom she had never
in her life exchanged a single word!

CHAPTER II

AN AFFAIR OF THE SEVENTIES

Having satisfied her obstinacy by sitting down on the seat of her choice, she might surely – one would think – have ended a mysteriously difficult situation by rising again and departing, of course with due dignity. But no! She could not! She wished to do so, but she could not command her limbs. She just sat there, in horridest torture, like a stoical fly on a pin – one of those flies that pretend that nothing hurts. The agony might have been prolonged to centuries had not an extremely startling and dramatic thing happened – the most startling and dramatic thing that ever happened either to James Ollerenshaw or to the young woman. James Ollerenshaw spoke, and I imagine that nobody was more surprised than James Ollerenshaw by his brief speech, which slipped out of him quite unawares. What he said was:

'Well, lass, how goes it, like?'

If the town could have heard him, the town would have rustled from boundary to boundary with agitated and delicious whisperings.

The young woman, instead of being justly incensed by this monstrous molestation from an aged villain who had not been introduced to her, gave a little jump (as though relieved from the spell of an enchantment), and then deliberately turned and faced Mr. Ollerenshaw. She also smiled, amid her roses.

'Very well indeed, thank you,' she replied, primly, but nicely.

Upon this, they both of them sought to recover – from an affair that had occurred in the late seventies.

In the late seventies James Ollerenshaw had been a young-old man of nearly thirty. He had had a stepbrother, much older and much poorer than himself, and the step-brother had died, leaving a daughter, named Susan, almost,

but not quite, in a state of indigence. The stepbrother and
James had not been on terms of effusive cordiality. But James
was perfectly ready to look after Susan, his stepniece. Susan,
aged seventeen years, was, however, not perfectly ready to be
looked after. She had a little money, and she earned a little (by
painting asters on toilet ware), and the chit was very rude to
her stepuncle. In less than a year she had married a youth of
twenty, who apparently had not in him even the rudiments of
worldly successfulness. James Ollerenshaw did his avuncular
duty by formally and grimly protesting against the marriage.
But what authority has a stepuncle? Susan defied him, with a
maximum of unforgettable impoliteness; and she went to live
with her husband at Longshaw, which is at the other end of
the Five Towns. The fact became public that a solemn quarrel
existed between James and Susan, and that each of them had
sworn not to speak until the other spoke. James would have
forgiven, if she had hinted at reconciliation. And, hard as it is
for youth to be in the wrong, Susan would have hinted at
reconciliation if James had not been so rich. The riches of
James offended Susan's independence. Not for millions would
she have exposed herself to the suspicion that she had broken
her oath because her stepuncle was a wealthy and childless
man. She was, of course, wrong. Nor was this her only
indiscretion. She was so ridiculously indiscreet as to influence
her husband in such a way that he actually succeeded in life.
Had James perceived them to be struggling in poverty, he
might conceivably have gone over to them and helped them,
in an orgy of forgiving charity. But the success of young
Rathbone falsified his predictions utterly, and was further, an
affront to him. Thus the quarrel slowly crystallised into a
permanent estrangement, a passive feud. Everybody got
thoroughly accustomed to it, and thought nothing of it, it
being a social phenomenon not at all unique of its kind in the
Five Towns. When fifteen years later, Rathbone died in mid-
career, people thought that the feud would end. But it did not.
James wrote a letter of condolence to his niece, and even sent it
to Longshaw by special messenger in the tramcar; but he had
not heard of the death until the day of the funeral, and Mrs
Rathbone did not reply to his letter. Her independence and
sensitiveness were again in the wrong. James did no more.

You could not expect him to have done more. Mrs. Rathbone, like many widows of successful men, was 'left poorly off.' But she 'managed.' Once, five years before the scene on the park terrace, Mrs Rathbone and James had encountered one another by hazard on the platform of Knype Railway Station. Destiny hesitated while Susan waited for James's recognition and James waited for Susan's recognition. Both of them waited too long. Destiny averted its head and drew back, and the relatives passed on their ways without speaking. James observed with interest a girl of twenty by Susan's side – her daughter. This daughter of Susan's was now sharing the park bench with him. Hence the hidden drama of their meeting, of his speech, of her reply.

'And what's your name, lass?'

'Helen.'

'Helen what?'

'Helen, great-stepuncle,' said she.

He laughed; and she laughed also. The fact was that he had been aware of her name vaguely. It had come to him, on the wind, or by some bird's wing, although none of his acquaintances had been courageous enough to speak to him about the affair of Susan for quite twenty years past. Longshaw is as far from Bursley, in some ways, as San Francisco from New York. There are people in Bursley who do not know the name of the Mayor of Longshaw – who make a point of not knowing it. Yet news travels even from Longshaw to Bursley, by mysterious channels; and Helen Rathbone's name had so travelled. James Ollerenshaw was glad that she was just Helen. He had been afraid that there might be something fancy between Helen and Rathbone – something expensive and aristocratic that went with her dress and her parasol. He illogically liked her for being called merely Helen – as if the credit were hers! Helen was an old Ollerenshaw name – his grandmother's (who had been attached to the household of Josiah Wedgwood), and his aunt's. Helen was historic in his mind. And, further, it could not be denied that Rathbone was a fine old Five Towns name too.

He was very illogical that afternoon; he threw over the principles of a lifetime, arguing from particulars to generals exactly like a girl. He had objected, always, to the expensive and the aristocratic. He was proud of his pure plebeian blood, as many plebeians are; he gloried in it. He disliked show, with a calm and deep aversion. He was a plain man with a simple, unostentatious taste for money. The difference between Helen's name and her ornamental raiment gave him pleasure in the name. But he had not been examining her for more than half a minute when he began to find pleasure in her rich clothes (rich, that is, to him!). Quite suddenly he, at the age of sixty, abandoned without an effort his dear prejudice against fine feathers, and began, for the first time, to take joy in sitting next to a pretty and well-dressed woman. And all this, not from any broad, philosophic perception that fine feathers have their proper part in the great scheme of cosmic evolution; but because the check dress suited her, and the heavy, voluptuous parasol suited her, and the long black gloves were inexplicably effective. Women grow old; women cease to learn; but men, never.

As for Helen, she liked him. She had liked him for five years, ever since her mother had pointed him out on the platform of Knype Railway station. She saw him closer now. He was older than she had been picturing him; indeed, the lines on his little, rather wizened face, and the minute sproutings of grey-white hair in certain spots on his reddish chin, where he had shaved himself badly, caused her somehow to feel quite sad. She thought of him as 'a dear old thing,' and then as 'a dear old darling.' Yes, old, very old! Nevertheless, she felt maternal towards him. She felt that she was much wiser than he was, and that she could teach him a great deal. She saw very clearly how wrong he and her mother had been, with their stupidly terrific quarrel; and the notion of all the happiness which he had missed, in his solitary, unfeminised, bachelor existence, nearly brought into her eyes tears of a quick and generous sympathy.

He, blind and shabby ancient, had no suspicion that his melancholy state and the notion of all the happiness he had missed had tinged with sorrow the heart within the frock, and added a dangerous humidity to the glance under the sunshade. It did not occur to him that he was an object of pity, nor that a vast store of knowledge was waiting to be poured into him. The aged, self-satisfied wag-beard imagined that he had conducted his career fairly well. He knew no one with whom he would have changed places. He regarded Helen as an extremely agreeable little thing, with her absurd air of being grown-up. Decidedly in five years she had tremendously altered. Five years ago she had been gawky. Now . . . Well, he was proud of her. She had called him great-stepuncle, thus conferring on him a sort of part-proprietorship in her; and he was proud of her. The captain of the bowling club came along, and James Ollerenshaw gave him just such a casual nod as he might have given to a person of no account. The nod seemed to say: 'Match this, if you can. It's mine, and there's nothing in the town to beat it. Mrs. Prockter herself hasn't got more style than this.' (Of this Mrs. Prockter, more later.)

Helen soon settled down into a condition of ease, which put an end to blushing. She knew she was admired.

'What are you doing i' Bosley?' James demanded.

'I'm living i' Bosley,' she retorted, smartly.

'Living here!' He stopped, and his hard old heart almost stopped too. If not in mourning, she was in semi-mourning. Surely Susan had not had the effrontery to die, away in Longshaw, without telling him!

'Mother has married again,' said Helen, lightly.

'Married!' He was staggered. The wind was knocked out of him.

'Yes. And gone to Canada!' Helen added.

You pick up your paper in the morning, and idly and slowly peruse the advertisements on the first page, forget it, eat some bacon, grumble at the youngest boy, open the paper, read the breach of promise case on page three, drop it, and ask your wife for more coffee – hot – glance at your letters again, then reopen the paper at the news page, and find that the Tsar of Russia has been murdered, and a few American cities tumbled to fragments by an earthquake – you know how you feel then. James Ollerenshaw felt like that. The captain of the bowling club, however, poising a bowl in his right hand, and waiting for James Ollerenshaw to leave his silken dalliance, saw nothing but an old man and a young woman sitting on a Corporation seat.

CHAPTER III

MARRYING OFF A MOTHER

'Yes,' said Helen Rathbone, 'mother fell in love. Don't you think it was funny?'

'That's as may be,' James Ollerenshaw replied, in his quality of the wiseacre who is accustomed to be sagacious on the least possible expenditure of words.

'We both thought it was awfully funny,' Helen said.

'Both? Who else is there?'

'Why, mother and I, of course! We used to laugh over it. You see, mother is a very simple creature. And she's only forty-four.'

'She's above forty-four,' James corrected.

'She *told* me she was thirty-nine five years ago,' Helen protested.

'Did she tell ye she was forty, four years ago?'

'No. At least, I don't remember.'

'Did she ever tell ye she was forty?'

'No.'

'Happen she's not such a simple creature as ye thought for, my lass,' observed James Ollerenshaw.

'You don't mean to infer,' said Helen, with cold dignity, 'that my *mother* would tell me a lie?'

'All as I mean is that Susan was above thirty-nine five years ago, and I can prove it. I had to get her birth certificate when her father died, and I fancy I've got it by me yet.' And his eyes added: 'So much for that point. One to me.'

Helen blushed and frowned, and looked up into the darkling heaven of her parasol; and then it occurred to her that her wisest plan would be to laugh. So she laughed. She laughed in almost precisely the same manner as James had heard Susan laugh thirty years previously, before love had come into Susan's life like a shell into a fortress, and finally blown their fragile relations all to pieces. A few minutes earlier the sight of great-stepuncle James had filled Helen with sadness, and he had not suspected it. Now her laugh filled James with sadness, and she did not suspect it. In his sadness, however, he was glad that she laughed so naturally, and that the sombre magnificence of her dress and her gloves and parasol did not prevent her from opening her rather large mouth and showing her teeth.

'It was just like mother to tell me fibs about her age,' said Helen, generously (it is always interesting to observe the transformation of a lie into a fib). 'And I shall write and tell her she's a horrid mean thing. I shall write to her this very night.'

'So Susan's gone and married again!' James murmured, reflectively.

Helen now definitely turned the whole of her mortal part towards James, so that she fronted him, and her feet were near his. He also turned, in response to this diplomatic advance, and leant his right elbow on the back of the seat, and his chin on his right palm. He put his left leg over his right leg, and thus his left foot swayed like a bird on a twig within an inch of Helen's flounce. The parasol covered the faces of the just and the unjust impartially.

'I suppose you don't know a farmer named Bratt that used to have a farm near Sneyd?' said Helen.

'I can't say as I do,' said James.

'Well, that's the man!' said Helen. 'He used to come to Longshaw cattle-market with sheep and things.'

'Sheep and things!' echoed James. 'What things?'

'Oh! I don't know,' said Helen, sharply. 'Sheep and things.'

'And what did your mother take to Longshaw cattle-market?' James inquired. 'I understood as she let lodgings.'

'Not since I've been a teacher,' said Helen, rather more sharply. 'Mother didn't take anything to the cattle-market. But you know our house was just close to the cattle-market.'

'No, I didn't,' said James, stoutly. 'I thought as it was in Aynsley Street.'

'Oh! that's years ago!' said Helen, shocked by his ignorance. 'We've lived in Sneyd Road for years – years.'

'I'll not deny it,' said James.

'The great fault of our house,' Helen proceeded, 'was that mother daren't stir out of it on cattle-market days.'

'Why not?'

'Cows!' said Helen. 'Mother simply can't look at a cow, and they were passing all the time.'

'She should ha' been thankful as it wasn't bulls,' James put in.

'But I mean bulls too!' exclaimed Helen. 'In fact, it was a bull that led to it.'

'What! Th' farmer saved her from a mad bull, and she fell in love with him? He's younger than her, I lay!'

'How did you know that?' Helen questioned. 'Besides, he isn't. They're just the same age.'

'Forty-four?' Perceiving delicious danger in the virgin's face, James continued before she could retort, 'I hope Susan wasn't gored?'

'You're quite wrong. You're jumping to conclusions,' said Helen, with an air of indulgence that would have been exasperating had it not been enchanting. 'Things don't happen like that except in novels.'

'I've never read a novel in my life,' James defended himself.

'Haven't you? How interesting!'

'But I've known a woman knocked down by a bull.'

'Well, anyhow, mother wasn't knocked down by a bull. But there was a mad bull running down the street; it had escaped from the market. And Mr. Bratt was walking home, and the bull was after him like a shot. Mother was looking out of the window, and she saw what was going on. So she rushed to the front door and opened it, and called to Mr. Bratt to run in and take shelter. And they only just got the door shut in time.'

'Bless us!' muttered James. 'And what next?'

'Why, I came home from school and found them having tea together.'

'And ninety year between them!' James reflected.

'Then Mr. Bratt called every week. He was a widower with no children.'

'It couldn't ha' been better,' said James.

'Oh yes, it could,' said Helen. 'Because I had the greatest difficulty in marrying them; in fact, at one time I thought I should never do it. I'm always in the right, and mother's always in the wrong. She admitted that for years. She's had to admit it. Yet she *would* go her own way. Nothing would ever cure mother.'

'She used to talk just like that of your grandfather,' said James. 'Susan always reckoned as she'd got more than her fair share of sense.'

'I don't think she thinks that now,' said Helen calmly, as if to say; 'At any rate I've cured her of *that*.' Then she went on; 'You see, Mr. Bratt had sold his farm – couldn't make it pay – and he was going out to Manitoba. He said he would stop in England. Mother said she wouldn't let him stop in England where he couldn't make a farm pay. She was quite right there,' Helen admitted, with careful justice. 'But then she said she wouldn't marry him and go out to Manitoba, because of leaving me alone here to look after myself! Can you imagine such a reason?'

James merely raised his head quickly several times. The gesture meant whatever Helen preferred that it should mean.

'The idea!' she continued. 'As if I hadn't looked after mother and kept her in order, and myself, too, for several years! No. She wouldn't marry him and go out there! And she wouldn't marry him and stay here! She actually began to talk all the usual conventional sort of stuff, you know – about how she had no right to marry again, and she didn't believe in second marriages, and about her duty to me. And so on. You know. I reasoned with her – I explained to her that probably she had another thirty years to live. I told her she was quite young. She *is*. And why should she make herself permanently miserable, *and* Mr. Bratt, *and* me, merely out of a quite mistaken sense of duty? No use! I tried everything I could. No use!'

'She was too much for ye?'

'Oh, *no!*' said Helen, condescendingly. 'I'd made up my *mind*. I arranged things with Mr. Bratt. He quite agreed with me. He took out a licence at the registrar's, and one Saturday morning – it had to be a Saturday, because I'm busy all the other days – I went out with mother to buy the meat and things for Sunday's dinner, and I got her into the registrar's office – and, well, there she was! Now, what do you think?'

'What?'

'Her last excuse was that she couldn't be married because she was wearing her third-best hat. Don't you think it's awfully funny?'

'That's as may be,' said James. 'When was all this?'

'Just recently,' Helen answered. 'They sailed from Glasgow last Thursday but two. And I'm expecting a letter by every post to say that they've arrived safely.'

'And Susan's left you to take care of yourself!'

'Now, please don't begin talking like mother,' Helen said, frigidly. 'I've certainly got less to take care of now than I had. Mother quite saw that. But what difficulty I had in getting her off, even after I'd safely married her! I had to promise that if I felt lonely I'd go and join them. But I shan't.'

'You won't?'

'No. I don't see myself on a farm in Manitoba. Do you?'

'I don't know as I do,' said James, examining her appearance, with a constant increase of his pride in it. 'So ye saw 'em off at Glasgow. I reckon she made a great fuss?'

'Fuss?'

'Cried.'

'Oh yes, of course.'

'Did you cry, miss?'

'Of course I cried,' said Helen, passionately, sitting up straight. 'Why do you ask such questions?'

'And us'll never see Susan again?'

'Of course I shall go over and *see* them,' said Helen. 'I only meant that I shouldn't go to stop. I daresay I shall go next year, in the holidays.'

CHAPTER IV

INVITATION TO TEA

They were most foolishly happy as they sat there on the bench, this man whose dim eyes ought to have been waiting placidly for the ship of death to appear above the horizon, and this young girl who imagined that she knew all about life and the world. When I say that they were foolishly happy, I of course mean that they were most wisely happy. Each of them, being gifted with common sense, and with a certain imperviousness to sentimentality which invariably accompanies common sense, they did not mar the present by regretting the tragic stupidity of a long estrangement; they did not mourn over wasted years that could not be recalled. It must be admitted, in favour of the Five Towns, that when its inhabitants spill milk they do not usually sit down on the pavement and adulterate the milk with their tears. They pass on. Such passing on is termed callous and coldhearted in the rest of England, which loves to sit down on pavements and weep into irretrievable milk.

Nor did Helen and her great-stepuncle mar the present by worrying about the future; it never occurred to them to be disturbed by the possibility that milk not already spilt might yet be spilt.

Helen had been momentarily saddened by private reflections upon what James Ollerenshaw had missed in his career; and James had been saddened, somewhat less, by reminiscences which had sprung out of Helen's laugh. But their melancholies had rapidly evaporated in the warmth of the unexpected encounter. They liked one another. She liked him because he was old and dry; and because he had a short laugh, and a cynical and even wicked gleam of the eye that pleased her; and because there was an occasional tone in his voice that struck her as deliciously masculine, ancient, and indulgent;

17

and because he had spoken to her first; and because his gaze
wandered with an admiring interest over her dress and up into
the dome of her sunshade; and because he put his chin in his
palm and leant his head towards her; and because the skin of
his hand was so crinkled and glossy. And he liked her because
she was exquisitely fresh and candid, so elegant, so violent and
complete a contrast to James Ollerenshaw; so absurdly sagacious and sure of herself, and perhaps because of a curve in her
cheek, and a mysterious suggestion of eternal enigma in her
large and liquid eye. When she looked right away from him,
as she sometimes did in the conversation, the outline of her
soft cheek, which drew in at the eye and swelled out again to
the temple, resembled a map of the coast of some smooth,
romantic country not mentioned in geographies. When she
looked *at* him – well, the effect on him astonished him; but it
enchanted him. He was discovering for the first time the soul
of a girl. If he was a little taken aback he is to be excused.
Younger men than he have been taken aback by that discovery. But James Ollerenshaw did not behave as a younger man
would have behaved. He was more like some one who,
having heard tell of the rose for sixty years, and having paid
no attention to rumour, suddenly sees a rose in early bloom.
At his age one knows how to treat a flower; one knows what
flowers are for.

It was no doubt this knowledge of what flowers are for that
almost led to the spilling of milk at the very moment when
milk-spilling seemed in a high degree improbable.

The conversation had left Susan and her caprices, and had
reached Helen and her solid wisdom.

'But you haven't told me what your're doing i' Bosley,' said
the old man.

'I've told you I'm living here.' said Helen. 'I've now been
living here for one week and one day. I'm teaching at the Park
Road Board School. I got transferred from Longshaw. I never
liked Longshaw, and I always like a change.'

'Yes,' said Ollerenshaw, judiciously, 'of the two I reckon as
Bosley is the frying-pan. So you're teaching up yonder?' He
jerked his elbow in the direction of the spacious and imposing
terra-cotta Board School, whose front looked on the eastern
gates of the park.

'What dost teach?'

'Oh, everything,' Helen replied.

'You must be very useful to 'em,' said James. 'What do they pay you for teaching everything?'

'Seventy-two pounds,' said Helen.

'A month? It 'ud be cheap at a hundred, lass; unless there's a whole crowd on ye as can teach everything. Can you sew?'

'Sew!' she exclaimed. 'I've given lessons in sewing for years. *And* cookery. *And* mathematics. I used to give evening lessons in mathematics at Longshaw secondary school.'

Great-stepuncle James gazed at her. It was useless for him to pretend to himself that he was not, secretly, struck all of a heap by the wonders of the living organism in front of him. He was. And this shows, though he was a wise man and an experienced, how ignorant he was of the world. But I do not think he was more ignorant of the world than most wise and experienced men are. He conceived Helen Rathbone as an extraordinary, an amazing creature. Nothing of the kind. There are simply thousands of agreeable and good girls who can accomplish herring-bone, omelettes, and simultaneous equations in a breath, as it were. They are all over the kingdom, and may be seen in the streets and lanes thereof about half-past eight in the morning and again about five o'clock in the evening. But the fact is not generally known. Only the stern and *blasé* members of School Boards or Education Committees know it. And they are so used to marvels that they make nothing of them.

However, James Ollerenshaw had no intention of striking his flag.

'Mathematics!' he murmured. 'I lay you can't tell me the interest on eighty-nine pounds for six months at four and a half per cent.'

Consols happened to be at eighty-nine that day.

Her lips curled. 'I'm really quite surprised you should encourage me to gamble,' said she. 'But I'll bet you a shilling I can. And I'll bet you one shilling against half-a-crown that I do it in my head, if you like. And if I lose I'll pay.'

She made a slight movement, and he noticed for the first time that she was carrying a small purse as black as her glove.

He hesitated, and then he proved what a wise and experienced man he was.

'No,' he said, 'I'll none bet ye, lass.'

He had struck his flag.

It is painful to be compelled to reinforce the old masculine statement that women have no sense of honour. But have they? Helen clearly saw that he had hauled down his flag. Yet did she cease firing? Not a bit. She gave him a shattering broadside, well knowing that he had surrendered. Her disregard of the ethics of warfare was deplorable.

'Two pounds and one half-penny – to the nearest farthing,' said she, a faint blush crimsoning her cheek.

Mr. Ollerenshaw glanced round at the bowling-green, where the captain in vain tried to catch his eye, and then at the groups of children playing on the lower terraces.

'I make no doubt ye can play the piano?' he remarked, when he had recovered.

'Certainly,' she replied. 'Not that we have to teach the piano. No! But it's understood, all the same, that one or another of us can play marches for the children to walk and drill to. In fact,' she added, 'for something less than thirty shillings a week we do pretty nearly everything, except build the schools. And soon they'll be expecting us to build the new schools in our spare time.' She spoke bitterly, as a native of the Congo Free State might refer to the late King of the Belgians.

'Thirty shillings a *wik*!' said James, acting with fine histrionic skill. 'I thought as you said seventy-two pounds a month!'

'Oh no, you didn't!' she protested, firmly. 'So don't try to tease me. I never joke about money. Money's a very serious thing.'

('Her's a chip o' th' owd block,' he told himself, delighted. When he explained matters to himself, and when he grew angry, he always employed the Five Towns dialect in its purest form.)

'You must be same as them hospital nurses,' he said, aloud. 'You do it because ye like it – for love on it, as they say.'

'Like it! I hate it. I hate any sort of work. What fun do you suppose there is in teaching endless stupid children, and stuffing in class-rooms all day, and correcting exercises and preparing sewing all night? Of course, they can't help being stupid. It's that that's so amazing. You can't help being kind to them – they're so stupid.'

'If ye didn't do that, what should ye do?' James inquired.

'I shouldn't do anything unless I was forced,' said she. 'I don't want to do anything, except enjoy myself – read, play the piano, pay visits, and have plenty of *really* nice clothes. Why should I want to do anything? I can tell you this – if I didn't need the money I'd never go inside that school again, or any other!'

She was heated.

'Dun ye mean to say,' he asked, with an ineffable intonation, 'that Susan and that there young farmer have gone gadding off to Canada and left you all alone with nothing?'

'Of course they haven't,' said Helen. 'Why, mother is the most generous old thing you can possibly imagine. She's left all her own income to me.'

'How much?'

'Well, it comes to rather over thirty shillings a week.'

'And can't you a single woman live on thirty shillings a *wik?* Bless us! I don't spend thirty shillings a wik myself.'

Helen raised her chin. 'A single woman can live on thirty shillings a week,' she said. 'But what about her frocks?'

'Well, what about her frocks?' he repeated.

'Well,' she said, 'I like frocks. It just happens that I can't do without frocks. It's just frocks that I work for; I spend nearly all I earn on them.' And her eyes, descending, seemed to say: 'Look at the present example.'

'Seventy pounds a year on ye clothes! Ye're not serious, lass?'

She looked at him coldly. 'I am serious,' she said.

Experienced as he was, he had never come across a fact so incredible as this fact. And the compulsion of believing it occupied his forces to such an extent that he had no force left to be wise. He did not observe the icy, darting challenge in her eye, and he ignored the danger in her voice.

'All as I can say is you ought to be ashamed o' yourself, lass!' he said, sharply. The reflection was blown out of him by the expansion of his feelings. Seventy pounds a year on clothes! . . . He too was serious.

Now, James Ollerenshaw was not the first person whom Helen's passion for clothes had driven into indiscretions. Her mother, for example, had done battle with that passion, and

had been defeated with heavy loss. A head-mistress and a
chairman of a School Board (a pompous coward) had also
suffered severely. And though Helen had been the victor, she
had not won without some injury to her nerves. Her cam-
paigns and conquests had left her, on this matter, 'touchy' – as
the word is used in the Five Towns.

'I shall be very much obliged if you will not speak to me in
that tone,' said she. 'Because I cannot permit it either from
you or any other man. When I venture to criticise your private
life I shall expect you to criticise mine – and not before. I don't
want to be rude, but I hope you understand, great-stepuncle.'

The milk was within the twentieth of an inch of the brim.
James Ollerenshaw blushed as red as Helen herself had blushed
at the beginning of their acquaintance. A girl, the daughter of
the chit Susan, to address him so! She had the incomparable
insolence of her mother. Yes, thirty years ago Susan had been
just as rude to him. But he was thirty years younger then; he
was not a sage of sixty then. He continued to blush. He was
raging. Indeed, it would be no exaggeration to assert that his
health was momentarily in peril. He glanced for an instant at
Helen, and saw that her nostrils were twitching. Then he
looked hurriedly away, and rose. The captain of the bowling
club excusably assumed that James was at length going to
attack the serious business of the day.

'Now, Mr. Ollerenshaw!' the captain called out; and his
tone implied, gently: 'Don't you think you've kept me
waiting long enough? Women are women; but a bowling-
match is a bowling-match.'

James turned his back on the captain, moved off, and then –
how can one explain it? He realised that in the last six words of
Helen's speech there had been a note, a hint, a mere nothing,
of softness, of regret for pain caused. He realised, further, the
great universal natural law that under any circumstances – no
matter what they may be – when any man – no matter who he
may be – differs from any pretty and well-dressed woman –
no matter who she may be – he is in the wrong. He saw that it
was useless for serious, logical, high-minded persons to
inveigh against the absurdity of this law, and to call it bad
names. The law of gravity is absurd and indefensible when
you fall downstairs; but you obey it.

He returned to Helen, who bravely met his eyes. 'I'm off home,' he said, hoarsely. 'It's my tea-time.'

'Good-afternoon,' she replied, with amiability.

'Happen you'll come along with me, like?'

The use of that word 'like' at the end of an interrogative sentence, in the Five Towns, is a subject upon which a book ought to be written; but not this history. The essential point to observe is that Helen got up from the bench and said, with adorable sweetness:

'Why, I shall be charmed to come!'

('What a perfect old darling he is!' she said to herself.)

CHAPTER V

A SALUTATION

As they walked down Moorthorne Road towards the town they certainly made a couple piquant enough, by reason of the excessive violence of the contrast between them, to amuse the eye of the beholder. A young and pretty woman who spends seventy pounds a year on her ornamentations, walking by the side of a little old man (she had the better of him by an inch) who had probably not spent seventy pounds on clothes in sixty years – such a spectacle must have drawn attention even in the least attentive of towns. And Bursley is far from the least attentive of towns. James and his great-stepniece had not got as far as the new Independent Chapel when it was known in St. Luke's Square, a long way farther on, that they were together; a tramcar had flown forward with the interesting fact. From that moment, of course, the news, which really was great news, spread itself over the town with the rapidity of a perfume; no corner could escape it. All James's innumerable tenants seemed to sniff it simultaneously. And that evening in the mouth of the entire town (I am licensing myself to a little poetical exaggeration) there was no word but the word 'Jimmy.'

Their converse, as they descended into the town, was not effective. It was, indeed, feeble. They had fought a brief but bitter duel, and James Ollerenshaw had been severely wounded. His dignity bled freely; he made, strange to say, scarcely any attempt to stanch the blood, which might have continued to flow for a considerable time had not a diversion occurred. (It is well known that the dignity will only bleed while you watch it. Avert your eyes, and it instantly dries up.) The diversion, apparently of a trifling character, had, in truth, an enormous importance, though the parties concerned did not perceive this till later. It consisted in the passing of Mrs.

24

Prockter and her stepson, Emanuel Prockter, up Duck Bank as James and Helen were passing down Duck Bank.

Mrs. Prockter (who by reason of the rare 'k' in her name regarded herself as the sole genuine in a district full of Proctors) may be described as the dowager of Bursley, the custodian of its respectability, and the summit of its social ladder. You could not climb higher than Mrs. Prockter. She lived at Hillport, and even in that haughty suburb there was none who dared palter with an invitation from Mrs. Prockter. She was stout and deliberate. She had waving flowers in her bonnet and pictures of flowers on her silken gown, and a grey mantle. Much of her figure preceded her as she walked. Her stepson had a tenor voice and a good tailor; his age was thirty.

Now, Mrs. Prockter was simply nothing to James Ollerenshaw. They knew each other by sight, but their orbits did not touch. James would have gone by Mrs. Prockter as indifferently as he would have gone by a police-man or a lamp-post. As for Emanuel, James held him in mild, benignant contempt. But when, as the two pairs approached one another, James perceived Emanuel fur-tively shifting his gold-headed cane from his right hand to his left, and then actually raise his hat to Helen, James swiftly lost his indifference. He also nearly lost his presence of mind. He was utterly unaccustomed to such crises. Despite his wealthy indifference to Mrs. Prockter, despite his distinguished scorn of Emanuel, despite the richness of Helen's attire, he was astounded, and deeply impressed, to learn that Helen had the acquaintance of people like the Prockters. Further, except at grave-sides, James Ollerenshaw had never in his life raised his hat. Hat-raising formed no part of his code of manners. In his soul he looked upon hat-raising as affected. He believed that all people who raised hats did so from a snobbish desire to put on airs. Hat-raising was rather like saying 'please,' only worse.

Happily, his was one of those strong, self-reliant natures that can, when there is no alternative, face the most fright-ful situations with unthumping heart. He kept his presence of mind, and decided in the fraction of a second what he must do. The faculty of instant decision is indispensable to safety in these swift-arising crises.

He raised his hat, praying that Helen would not stop to speak. Not gracefully, not with the beauteous curves of an Emanuel did he raise his hat – but he raised it. His prayer was answered.

'There!' his chest said to Helen. 'If you thought I didn't know how to behave to your conceited acquaintances, you were mistaken.'

And his casual, roving eye pretended that hat-raising was simply the most ordinary thing on earth.

Such was the disturbing incident which ended the bleeding of his dignity. In order to keep up the pretence that hat-raising was a normal function of his daily life he was obliged to talk freely; and he did talk freely. But neither he nor Helen said a word as to the Prockters.

CHAPTER VI

MRS. BUTT'S DEPARTURE

James Ollerenshaw's house was within a few hundred yards of the top of Trafalgar Road, on the way from Bursley to Hanbridge. I may not indicate the exact house, but I can scarcely conceal that it lay between Nos. 160 and 180, on the left as you go up. It was one of the oldest houses in the street, and though bullied into insignificance by sundry detached and semi-detached villas opposite – palaces occupied by reckless persons who think nothing of paying sixty or even sixty-five pounds a year for rent alone – it kept a certain individuality and distinction because it had been conscientiously built of good brick before English domestic architecture had lost trace of the Georgian style. First you went up two white steps (white in theory), through a little gate in a wrought-iron railing painted the colour of peas after they have been cooked in a bad restaurant. You then found yourself in a little front yard, twelve feet in width (the whole width of the house) by six feet in depth. The yard was paved with large square Indian-red tiles, except a tiny circle in the midst bordered with black-currant-coloured tiles set endwise with a scolloped edge. This magical circle contained earth, and in the centre of it was a rhododendron bush which, having fallen into lazy habits, had forgotten the art of flowering. Its leaves were a most pessimistic version of the tint of the railing.

The façade of the house comprised three windows and a door – that is to say, a window and a door on the ground floor and two windows above. The brickwork was assuredly admirable; James had it 'pointed' every few years. Over the windows the bricks, of special shapes, were arranged as in a flat arch, with a keystone that jutted slightly. The panes of the windows were numerous and small; inside, on the sashes, lay long thin scarlet sausages of red cloth and sawdust, to keep out

27

the draughts. The door was divided into eight small panels with elaborate beadings, and over it was a delicate fanlight – one of about a score in Bursley – to remind the observer of a lost elegance. Between the fanlight and the upstairs window exactly above it was a rusty iron plaque, with vestiges in gilt of the word 'Phoenix.' It had been put there when fire insurance had still the fancied charm of novelty. At the extremity of the façade farthest from the door a spout came down from the blue-slate roof. This spout began with a bold curve from the projecting horizontal spout under the eaves, and made another curve at the ground into a hollow earthen-ware grid with very tiny holes.

Helen looked delicious in the yard, gazing pensively at the slothful rhododendron while James Ollerenshaw opened his door. She was seen by two electric cars-full of people, for although James's latchkey was very highly polished and the lock well oiled, he never succeeded in opening his door at the first attempt. It was a capricious door. You could not be sure of opening it any more than Beau Brummel could be sure of tying his cravat. It was a muse that had to be wooed.

But when it did open you perceived that there were no half measures about that door, for it let you straight into the house. To open it was like taking down part of the wall. No lobby, hall, or vestibule behind that door! One instant you were in the yard, the next you were in the middle of the sitting-room, and through a doorway at the back of the sitting-room you could see the kitchen, and beyond that the scullery, and beyond that a back yard with a whitewashed wall.

James Ollerenshaw went in first, leaving Helen to follow. He had learnt much in the previous hour, but there were still one or two odd things left for him to learn.

'Ah!' he breathed, shut the door, and hung up his hard hat on the inner face of it. 'Sit ye down, lass.'

So she sat her down. It must be said that she looked as if she had made a mistake and got on to the wrong side of Trafalgar-road. The sitting-room was a crowded and shabby little apartment (though clean). There was a list carpet over the middle of the floor, which was tiled, and in the middle of the carpet a small square table with flap-sides. On this table was a full-rigged ship on a stormy sea in a glass box, some resin, a large stone bottle of ink, a ready reckoner, Whitaker's Almanack (paper edition), a foot-rule, and a bright brass candlestick. Above the table there hung from the ceiling a string with a ball of fringed paper, designed for the amusement of flies. At the window was a flat desk, on which were transacted the affairs of Mr. Ollerenshaw. When he stationed himself at it in the seat of custom and of judgment, defaulting tenants, twirling caps or twisting aprons, had a fine view of the left side of his face. He usually talked to them while staring out of the window. Before this desk was a Windsor chair. There were eight other Windsor chairs in the room – Helen was sitting on one that had not been sat upon for years and years – a teeming but idle population of chairs. A horse-hair arm-chair seemed to be the sultan of the seraglio of chairs. Opposite the window a modern sideboard, which might have cost two-nineteen-six when new, completed the tale of furniture. The general impression was one of fulness; the low ceiling, and the immense harvest of over-blown blue roses which climbed luxuriantly up the walls, intensified this effect. The mantelpiece was crammed with brass ornaments, and there were two complete sets of brass fire-irons in the brass fender. Above the mantelpiece a looking-glass, in a wan frame of bird's-eye maple, with rounded corners, reflected Helen's hat.

Helen abandoned the Windsor chair and tried the arm-chair, and then stood up.

'Which chair do you recommend?' she asked, nicely.

'Bless ye, child! I never sit here, except at th' desk. I sit in the kitchen.'

A peculiarity of houses in the Five Towns is that rooms are seldom called by their right names. It is a point of honour, among the self-respecting and industrious classes, to prepare a room elaborately for a certain purpose, and then not to use it for that purpose. Thus James Ollerenshaw's sitting-room, though surely few apartments could show more facilities than it showed for sitting, was not used as a sitting-room, but as an office. The kitchen, though it contained a range, was not used as a kitchen, but as a sitting-room. The scullery, though it had no range, was filled with a gas cooking-stove and used as a kitchen. And the back yard was used as a scullery. This arrangement never struck anybody as singular; it did not strike even Helen as singular. Her mother's house had exhibited the same oddness until she reorganised it. If James Ollerenshaw had not needed an office, his sitting-room would have languished in desuetude. The fact is that the thrifty inhabitants of the Five Towns save a room as they save money. If they have an income of six rooms they will live on five, or rather in five, and thereby take pride to themselves.

Somewhat nervous, James feigned to glance at the rent books on the desk.

Helen's eye swept the room. 'I suppose you have a good servant?' she said.

'I have a woman as comes in,' said James. 'But her isn't in th' house at the moment.'

This latter statement was a wilful untruth on James's part. He had distinctly caught a glimpse of Mrs. Butt's figure as he entered.

'Well,' said Helen, kindly, 'it's quite nice, I'm sure. You must be very comfortable – for a man. But, of course, one can see at once that no woman lives here.'

'How?' he demanded naïvely.

'Oh,' she answered, 'I don't know. But one can.'

'Dost mean to say as it isn't clean, lass?'

'The 'brasses' are very clean,' said Helen.

Such astonishing virtuosity in the art of innuendo is the privilege of one sex only.

'Come into th' kitchen, lass,' said James, after he had smiled into a corner of the room, 'and take off them gloves and things.'

'But, great-stepuncle, I can't stay.'

'You'll stop for tea,' said he, firmly, 'or my name isn't James Ollerenshaw.'

He preceded her into the kitchen. The door between the kitchen and the scullery was half-closed; in the aperture he again had a momentary, but distinct, glimpse of the eye of Mrs. Butt.

'I do like this room,' said Helen, enthusiastically.

'Uninterrupted view o' th' back yard,' said Ollerenshaw. 'Sit ye down, lass.'

He indicated an article of furniture which stood in front of the range, at a distance of perhaps six feet from it, cutting the room in half. This contrivance may be called a sofa, or it may be called a couch; but it can only be properly described by the Midland word for it – squab. No other term is sufficiently expressive. Its seat – five feet by two – was very broad and very low, and it had a steep, high back and sides. All its angles were right angles. It was everywhere comfortably padded; it yielded everywhere to firm pressure; and it was covered with a grey and green striped stuff. You could not sit on that squab and be in a draught; yet behind it, lest the impossible should arrive, was a heavy curtain, hung on an iron rod which crossed the room from wall to wall. Not much imagination was needed to realise the joy and ecstasy of losing yourself on that squab on a winter afternoon, with the range fire roaring in your face, and the curtain drawn abaft.

Helen assumed the mathematical centre of the squab, and began to arrange her skirts in cascading folds; she had posed her parasol in a corner of it, as though the squab had been a railway carriage, which, indeed, it did somewhat resemble.

'By the way, lass, what's that as swishes?' James demanded.

'What's what?'

'What's that as swishes?'

She looked puzzled for an instant, then laughed – a frank, gay laugh, light and bright as aluminium, such as the kitchen had never before heard.

'Oh!' she said. 'It's my new silk petticoat, I suppose. You mean that?' She brusquely moved her limbs, reproducing the unique and delicious rustle of concealed silk.

'Aye!' ejaculated the old man, 'I mean that.'

'Yes. It's my silk petticoat. Do you like it?'

'I havena' seen it, lass.'

She bent down, and lifted the hem of her dress just two inches – the discreetest, the modestest gesture. He had a transient vision of something fair – it was gone again.

'I don't know as I dislike it,' said he.

He was standing facing her, his back to the range, and his head on a level with the high narrow mantelpiece, upon which glittered a row of small tin canisters. Suddenly he turned to the corner to the right of the range, where, next to an oak cupboard, a velvet Turkish smoking-cap depended from a nail. He put on the cap, of which the long tassel curved down to his ear. Then he faced her again, putting his hands behind him, and raising himself at intervals on his small, well-polished toes. She lifted her two hands simultaneously to her head, and began to draw pins from her hat, which pins she placed one after another between her lips. Then she lowered the hat carefully from her head, and transfixed it anew with the pins.

'Will you mind hanging it on that nail?' she requested.

He took it, as though it had been of glass, and hung it on the nail.

Without her hat she looked as if she lived there, a jewel in a pipe-case. She appeared to be just as much at home as he was. And they were so at home together that there was no further necessity to strain after a continuous conversation. With a vague smile she gazed round and about, at the warm, cracked, smooth red tiles of the floor; at the painted green walls, at a Windsor chair near the cupboard – a solitary chair that had evidently been misunderstood by the large family of relatives in the other room and sent into exile; at the pair of bellows that hung on the wall above the chair, and the rich gaudiness of the grocer's almanac above the bellows; at the tea-table, with its coarse grey cloth and thick crockery spread beneath the window.

'So you have all your meals here?' she ventured.

'Ay,' he said. 'I have what I call my meals here.'

'Why,' she cried, 'don't you enjoy them?'

'I eat 'em,' he said.

'What time do you have tea?' she inquired.

'Four o'clock,' said he. 'Sharp!'

'But it's a quarter to, now!' she exclaimed, pointing to a clock with weights at the end of brass chains and a long pendulum. 'And didn't you say your servant was out?'

'Ay,' he mysteriously lied. 'Her's out. But her'll come back. Happen her's gone to get a bit o' fish or something.'

'Fish! Do you always have fish for tea?'

'I have what I'm given,' he replied. 'I fancy a snack for my tea. Something tasty, ye know.'

'Why,' she said, 'you're just like me. I adore tea. I'd sooner have tea than any other meal of the day. But I never yet knew a servant who could get something tasty every day. Of course, it's quite easy if you know how to do it; but servants don't –

that is to say, as a rule – but I expect you've got a very good one.'

'So-so!' James murmured. 'The trouble with servants is that they always think that if you like a thing one day you'll like the same thing every day for the next three years.'

'Ay,' he said, drily. 'I used to like a kidney, but it's more than three years ago.' He stuck his lips out, and raised himself higher than ever on his toes.

He did not laugh. But she laughed, almost boisterously.

'I can't help telling you,' she said, 'you're perfectly lovely, great-stepuncle. Are we both going to drink out of the same cup?' In such manner did the current of her talk gyrate and turn corners.

He approached the cupboard.

'No, no!' She sprang up. 'Let me. I'll do that, as the servant is so long.'

And she opened the cupboard. Among a miscellany of crocks therein was a blue-and-white cup and saucer, and a plate to match underneath it, that seemed out of place there. She lifted down the pile.

'Steady on!' he counselled her. 'Why dun you choose that?'

'Because I like it,' she replied, simply.

He was silenced. 'That's a bit o' real Spode,' he said, as she put it on the table and dusted the several pieces with a corner of the tablecloth.

'It won't be in any danger,' she retorted, 'until it comes to be washed up. So I'll stop afterwards and wash it up myself. There!'

'Now you can't find the teaspoons, miss!' he challenged her.

'I think I can,' she said.

She raised the table cloth at the end, discovered the knob of a drawer, and opened it. And, surely, there were teaspoons.

'Can't I just take a peep into the scullery?' she begged, with a bewitching supplication. 'I won't stop. It's nearly time your servant was back if she's always so dreadfully prompt as you say. I won't touch anything. Servants are so silly. They always think one wants to interfere with them.'

Without waiting for James's permission, she burst youthfully into the scullery.

'Oh,' she exclaimed, 'there's someone here!'

Of course there was. There was Mrs. Butt.

Although the part played by Mrs. Butt in the drama was vehement and momentous, it was nevertheless so brief that a description of Mrs. Butt is hardly called for. Suffice it to say that she had so much waist as to have no waist, and that she possessed both a beard and a moustache. This curt catalogue of her charms is unfair to her; but Mrs. Butt was ever the victim of unfairness.

James Ollerenshaw looked audaciously in at the door. 'It's Mrs. Butt,' said he. 'Us thought as ye were out.'

'Good-afternoon, Mrs. Butt,' Helen began, with candid pleasantness.

A pause.

'Good-afternoon, miss.'

'And what have you got for uncle's tea to-day? Something tasty?'

'I've got this,' said Mrs. Butt, with candid unpleasantness. And she pointed to an oblate spheroid, the colour of brick, but smoother, which lay on a plate near the gas-stove. It was a kidney.

'H'm!' – from James.

'It's not cooked yet, I see,' Helen observed. 'And —'

The cook finished her remark.

'No, miss, it's not cooked,' said Mrs. Butt. 'To tell ye the honest truth, miss, I've been learning, 'stead o' cooking this 'ere kidney.' She picked up the kidney in her pudding-like hand and gazed at it. 'I'm glad the brasses is clean, miss, at any rate, though the house *does* look as though there was no woman about the place, and servants *are* silly. I'm thankful to Heaven as the brasses is clean. Come into my scullery, and welcome.'

She ceased, still holding up the kidney.

'H'm!' – from Uncle James.

This repeated remark of his seemed to rouse the fury in her. 'You may 'h'm' Mester Ollerenshaw,' she glared at him. 'You may 'h'm' as much as yo'n a mind.' Then to Helen: 'Come in, miss; come in. Don't be afraid of servants.' And finally, with a striking instinct for theatrical effect: 'But I go out!'

She flung the innocent and yielding kidney to the floor, snatched up a bonnet, cast off her apron, and departed.

'There!' said James Ollerenshaw. 'You've done it!'

CHAPTER VII

THE NEW COOK

Ten minutes later Mr. James Ollerenshaw stood alone in his kitchen-sitting-room. And he gazed at the door between the kitchen-sitting-room and the scullery. This door was shut; that is to say, it was nearly shut. He had been turned out of his scullery; not with violence – or, rather, with a sort of sweet violence that he liked, and that had never before been administered to him by any human soul. An afternoon highly adventurous – an afternoon on which he had permitted himself to be insulted, with worse than impunity to the insulter, by the childish daughter of that chit Susan – an afternoon on which he had raised his hat to Mrs. Prockter – a Saturday afternoon on which he had foregone, on account of a woman, his customary match at bowls – this afternoon was drawing to a close in a manner which piled thrilling event on thrilling event.

Mrs. Butt had departed. For unnumbered years Mrs. Butt had miscooked his meals. The little house was almost inconceivable without Mrs. Butt. And Mrs. Butt had departed. Already he missed her as one misses an ancient and supersensitive corn – if the simile may be permitted to one; it is a simile not quite nice, but, then, Mrs. Butt was not quite nice either. The fault was not hers; she was born so.

The dropping of the kidney with a *plop*, by Mrs. Butt, on the hard, unsympathetic floor of the scullery, had constituted an extremely dramatic moment in three lives. Certainly Mrs. Butt possessed a wondrous instinct for theatrical effect. Helen, on the contrary, seemed to possess none. She had advanced nonchalantly towards the kidney, and delicately picked it up between finger and thumb, and turned it over, and then put it on a plate.

'That's a veal kidney,' she had observed.

'Art sure it isn't a sheep's kidney, lass?' James had asked, carefully imitating Helen's nonchalance.

'Yes,' she had said. 'I gather you are not passionately fond of kidneys, great-stepuncle?' she had asked.

'I was once. What art going to do, lass?'

'I'm going to get our tea,' she said.

At the words, *our* tea, the antique James Ollerenshaw, who had never thought to have such a sensation again, was most distinctly conscious of an agreeable, somewhat disturbing sensation of being tickled in the small of his back.

'Well,' he had asked her, 'what can I do?'

'You can go out,' she had replied. 'Wouldn't it be a good thing for you to go out for a walk? Tea will be ready at half-past four.'

'I go for no walk,' he said, positively. . . .

'Yes, that's all right,' she had murmured, but not in response to his flat refusal to obey her. She had been opening the double cupboard and the five drawers which constituted the receptacles of the scullery-larder; she had been spying out the riches and the poverty of the establishment. Then she had turned to him, and, instead of engaging him in battle, she had just smiled at him, and said: 'Very well. As you wish. But do go into the front room, at any rate.'

And there he was in the middle room, the kitchen, listening to her movements behind the door. He heard the running of water, and then the mild explosion of lighting the second ring of the gas-stove; the first had been lighted by Mrs. Butt. Then he heard nothing whatever for years, and when he looked at the clock it was fourteen minutes past four. In the act of looking at the clock, his eye had to traverse the region of the sofa. On the sofa were one parasol and two gloves. Astonishing, singular, disconcerting, how those articles – which, after all, bore no kind of resemblance to any style of furniture or hangings – seemed, nevertheless, to refurnish the room, to give the room an air of being thickly inhabited which it never had before!

Then she burst into the kitchen unexpectedly, with a swish of silk that was like the retreat of waves down the shingle of some Atlantic shore.

'My dear uncle,' she protested, 'please do make yourself scarce. You are in my way, and I'm very busy.'

She went to the cupboard and snatched at some plates, two of which she dropped on the table, and three of which she took into the kitchen.

'Have ye got all as ye want?' he questioned her politely, anxious to be of assistance.

'Everything!' she answered, positively, and with just the least hint of an intention to crush him.

'Have ye indeed!'

He did not utter this exclamation aloud; but with it he applied balm to his secret breast. For he still remembered, being an old man, her crushing him in the park, and the peril of another crushing roused the male in him. And it was with a sardonic and cruel satisfaction that he applied such balm to his secret breast. The truth was, he knew that she had not got all she wanted. He knew that, despite her extraordinary capableness (of which she was rather vain), despite her ability to calculate mentally the interest on eighty-nine pounds for six months at four-and-a-half per cent., she could not possibly prepare the tea without coming to him and confessing to him that she had been mistaken, and that she had *not* got everything she wanted. She would be compelled to humble herself before him – were it ever so little. He was a hard old man, and the prospect of this humbling gave him pleasure (I regret to say).

You cannot have tea without tea-leaves; and James Ollerenshaw kept the tea-leaves in a tea-caddy, locked, in his front room. He had an extravagant taste in tea. He fancied China tea; and he fancied China tea that cost five shillings a pound. He was the last person to leave China tea at five shillings a pound to the economic prudence of a Mrs. Butt. Every day Mrs. Butt brought to him the teapot (warmed) and a teaspoon, and he unlocked the tea-caddy, dispensed the right quantity of tea, and relocked the tea-caddy.

There was no other tea in the house. So with a merry heart the callous fellow (shamefully delighting in the imminent downfall of a fellow-creature – and that a woman!) went into the front room as he had been bidden. On one of the family of chairs, in a corner, was a black octagonal case. He opened this case, which was not locked, and drew from it a concertina, all inlaid with mother-of-pearl. Then he went to the desk, and

from under a pile of rent books he extracted several pieces of
music, and selected one. This selected piece he reared up on the
mantelpiece against two brass candlesticks. It was obvious,
from the certainty and ease of his movements, that he had the
habit of lodging pieces of music against those two brass
candlesticks. The music bore the illustrious name of George
Frederick Handel.

Then he put on a pair of spectacles which were lying on the
mantelpiece, and balanced them on the end of his nose. Finally
he adjusted his little hands to the straps of the concertina. You
might imagine that he would instantly dissolve into melody.
Not at all. He glanced at the page of music first through his
spectacles, and then, bending forward his head, *over* his spectacles. Then he put down the concertina, gingerly, on a chair, and
moved the music half-an-inch (perhaps five-eighths) to the left.
He resumed the concertina, and was on the very point of song,
when he put down the concertina for the second time, and
moved the tassel of his Turkish cap from the neighbourhood of
his left ear to the neighbourhood of his right ear. Then, with a
cough, he resumed the concertina once more, and embarked
upon the interpretation of Handel.

It was the Hallelujah Chorus.

Any surprise which the musical reader may feel on hearing
that James Ollerenshaw was equal to performing the Hallelujah
Chorus on a concertina (even one inlaid with mother-of-pearl)
argues on the part of that reader an imperfect acquaintance with
the Five Towns. In the Five Towns there are (among piano
scorners) two musical instruments, the concertina and the
cornet. And the Five Towns would like to see the composer
clever enough to compose a piece of music that cannot be
arranged for either of these instruments. It is conceivable that
Beethoven imagined, when he wrote the last movement of the
C Minor Symphony, that he had produced a work which it
would be impossible to arrange for cornet solo. But if he did he
imagined a vain thing. In the Five Towns, where the taste for
classical music is highly developed, the C Minor Symphony on
a single cornet is as common as 'Robin Adair' on a full brass
band.

James Ollerenshaw played the Hallelujah Chorus with much
feeling and expression. He understood the Hallelujah Chorus to

its profoundest depths; which was not surprising in view of the fact that he had been playing it regularly since before Helen was born. (The unfading charm of classical music is that you never tire of it.)

Nevertheless, the grandeur of his interpretation of the Hallelujah Chorus appeared to produce no effect whatever in the scullery; neither alarm nor ecstasy! And presently, in the midst of a brief pianissimo passage, James's sensitive ear caught the distant sound of chopping, which quite marred the soft tenderness at which he had been aiming. He stopped abruptly. The sound of chopping intrigued his curiosity. What could she be chopping? He advanced cautiously to the door-way; he had left the door open. The other door – between the kitchen and the scullery – which had previously been closed, was now open, so that he could see from the front room into the scullery. His eager, inquisitive glance noted a plate of beautiful bread and butter on the tea-table in the kitchen.

She was chopping the kidney. Utterly absorbed in her task, she had no suspicion that she was being overlooked. After the chopping of the kidney, James witnessed a series of operations the key to whose significance he could not find.

She put a flat pan over the gas, and then took it off again. Then she picked up an egg, broke it into a coffee-cup, and instantly poured it out of the coffee-cup into a basin. She did the same to another egg, and yet another. Four eggs! The entire household stock of eggs! It was terrible. Four eggs and a kidney among two people! He could not divine what she was at.

Then she got some butter on the end of a knife and dropped it into the saucepan, and put the saucepan over the gas; and then poured the plateful of kidney-shreds into the saucepan. Then she began furiously to beat the four eggs with a fork, glancing into the saucepan frequently, and coaxing it with little touches. Then the kidney-shreds raised a sound of frizzling, and bang into the saucepan went the contents of the basin. All the time she had held her hands and her implements and utensils away from her as much as possible, doubtless out of consideration for her frock; not an inch of apron was she wearing. Now she leant over the gas-stove, fork in hand, and made baffling motions inside the saucepan with the fork; and while doing so she stretched forth her left hand, obtained some salt, and sprinkled the saucepan therewith. The business seemed to be exquisitely delicate and breathless. Her face was sternly set, as though the fate of continents depended on her nerve and audacity in this tremendous crisis. But what she was doing to the interior of the saucepan James Ollerenshaw could not comprehend. She stroked it with a long gesture; she tickled it, she stroked it in a different direction; she lifted it and folded it on itself.

Anyhow, he knew it was not scrambled eggs; because you have to stir scrambled eggs without ceasing.

Then she stopped, and stood quite still, regarding the saucepan.

'You've watched me quite long enough,' she said, without moving her head. She must have known all the time that he was there.

So he shuffled away, and glanced out of the window at the stir and traffic of Trafalgar-road.

'Tea's ready,' she said.

He went into the kitchen, smiling, enchanted, but disturbed. She had not come to him and confessed that she could not make tea without tea-leaves. Yet there was the tea-pot steaming and puffing on the table!

CHAPTER VIII

OMELETTE

The mystery lay on a plate in the middle of the table. In colour it resembled scrambled eggs, except that it was tinted a more brownish, or coppery, gold rather like a first-class York-shire pudding. He suspected for an instant that it might be a Yorkshire pudding according to the new-fangled recipe of Board Schools. But four eggs! No! He was sure that so small a quantity of Yorkshire pudding could not possibly have required four eggs.

He picked up the teapot, after his manner, and was in the act of pouring, when she struck him into immobility with a loud cry:

'Milk first!'

He understood that she had a caprice for pouring the tea on the top of the milk instead of the milk on the top of the tea.

'What difference does it make?' he demanded, defiantly.

'What!' she cried again. 'You think yourself a great author-ity on China tea, and yet you don't know that milk ought to be poured in first! Why, it makes quite a different taste!'

How in the name of Confucius did she know that he thought himself a great authority on China tea?

'Here!' she said. 'If you don't mind, I'll pour out the tea. Thank you. Help yourself to this.' She pointed to the mystery. 'It must be eaten while it's hot, or it's worse than useless.'

'What is it?' he asked, with false calm.

'It's a kidney omelette,' she replied.

'Omelette!' he repeated, rather at a loss. He had never tasted an omelette; he had never seen an omelette. Omelettes form no part of the domestic cuisine of England. 'Omelette!' he repeated. How was he familiar with the word the word which conveyed nothing to his mind? Then he remembered: 'You can't make an omelette without breaking eggs.' Of

41

course she had broken eggs. She had broken four eggs she had broken the entire household stock of eggs. And he had employed that proverb scores, hundreds of times! It was one of half-a-dozen favourite proverbs which he flung at the less sagacious and prudent of his tenants. And yet it had never occurred to him to wonder what an omelette was! Now he knew. At any rate, he knew what it looked like; and he was shortly to know what it tasted like.

'Yes,' she said. 'Cut it with the knife. Don't be frightened of it. You'll eat *it*; it won't eat you. And please give me very little. I ate a quarter of a pound of chocolates after dinner.'

He conveyed one-third of the confection to his plate, and about a sixth to hers.

And he tasted just a morsel, with a dash of kidney in the centre of it, on the end of his fork. He was not aware of the fact, but that was the decisive moment of his life sixty though he was!

Had she really made this marvel, this dream, this idyll, this indescribable bliss, out of four common fresh eggs and a veal kidney that Mrs. Butt had dropped on the floor? He had come to loathe kidney. He had almost come to swearing that no manifestation or incarnation of kidney should ever again pass between his excellent teeth. And now he was ravished, rapt away on the wings of paradisaical ecstasy by a something that consisted of kidney and a few eggs. This omelette had all the finer and nobler qualities of Yorkshire pudding and scrambled eggs combined, together with others beyond the ken of his greedy fancy. Yes, he was a greedy man. He knew he was greedy. He was a greedy man whose evil passion had providentially been kept in check for over a quarter of a century by the gross unskilfulness, the appalling monotony, of a Mrs. Butt. Could it be that there existed women, light and light-handed creatures, creatures of originality and resource, who were capable of producing prodigies like this kidney omelette, on the spur of the moment? Evidently! Helen existed. And the whole omelette, from the melting of the butter to the final steady glance into the saucepan, had not occupied her more than six minutes at most. She had tossed it off as he might have tossed off a receipt for a week's rent. And the exquisite thought in his mind, the thought of penetrating sweetness,

was that whence this delicacy had come, other and even rarer
delicacies might have come. All his past life seemed to him to
be a miserable waste of gloomy and joyless years.

'Do you like it?' she inquired.

He paused, as though reflecting whether he liked it or not.
'Ay,' he said, judicially, 'it's none so bad. I could do a bit more
o' that.'

'Well,' she urged him, 'do help yourself. Take it all. I shan't
eat any more.'

'Sure?' he said, trembling lest she might change her mind.

Then he ate the remaining half of the omelette, making
five-sixths in all. He glanced at her surreptitiously, in her fine
dress, on which was not a single splash or stain. He might
have known that so extraordinary and exotic a female person
would not concoct anything so trite as a Yorkshire pudding or
scrambled eggs.

Not till the omelette was an affair of the past (so far as his
plate was concerned) did he begin to attend to his tea his tea
which sustained a mystery as curious as, and decidedly more
sinister than, the mystery of the omelette.

He stared into the cup; then, to use the Five Towns phrase,
he supped it up.

There could be no doubt; it was his special China tea. It had
a peculiar flavour (owing, perhaps, to the precedence given to
milk), but it was incontestably his guarded and locked tea.
How had she got it?

'Where didst find this tea, lass?' he asked.

'In the little corner cupboard in the scullery,' she said. 'I'd
no idea that people drank such good China tea in Bursley.'

'Ah!' he observed, concealing his concern under a mask of
irony, 'China tea was drunk i' Bursley afore your time.'

'Mother would only drink Ceylon,' said she.

'That doesna' surprise me,' said he, as if to imply that no
vagary on the part of Susan could surprise him. And he
proceeded, reflectively: 'In th' corner cupboard, sayst tha?'

'Yes, in a large tin box.'

A large tin box. This news was over-whelming. He rose
abruptly and went into the scullery. Indubitably there was a
large tin box, pretty nearly half full of his guarded tea, in the
corner cupboard.

He returned, the illusion of half a lifetime shattered. 'That there woman was a thief!' he announced.

'What woman?'

'Mrs. Butt'

And he explained to Helen all his elaborate precautions for the preservation of his China tea. Helen was wholly sympathetic. The utter correctness of her attitude towards Mrs. Butt was balm to him. Only one theory was conceivable. The wretched woman must have had a key to his caddy. During his absence from the house she must have calmly helped herself to tea at five shillings a pound a spoonful or so at a time. Doubtless she made tea for her private consumption exactly when she chose. It was even possible that she walked off from time to time with quantities of tea to her own home. And he who thought himself so clever, so much cleverer than a servant!

'You can't have her back, as she isn't honest, even if she comes back,' said Helen.

'Oh, her won't come back,' said James. 'Fact is, I've had difficulties with her for a long time now.'

'Then what shall you do, my poor dear uncle?'

'Nay,' said he, 'I mun ask you that. It was you as was th' cause of her going.'

'Oh, uncle!' she exclaimed, laughing. 'How can you say such a thing?' And she added, seriously: 'You can't be expected to cook for yourself, can you? And as for getting a new one —'

He noticed with satisfaction that she had taken to calling him simply uncle, instead of great-stepuncle.

'A new 'un!' he muttered grimly, and sighed in despair.

'I shall stay and look after your supper,' she said, brightly.

'Yes, and what about to-morrow?' He grew gloomier.

'To-morrow's Sunday. I'll come to-morrow, for breakfast.'

'Yes, and what about Monday?' His gloom was not easily to be dispersed.

'I'll come on Monday,' she replied, with increasing cheerfulness.

'But your school, where ye teach everything, lass?'

'Of course, I shall give up school,' said she, 'at once. They must do without me. It will mean promotion for someone. I can't bother about giving proper notice. Supposing you had been dangerously ill, I should have come, and they would have managed without me. Therefore, they *can* manage without me. Therefore, they must.'

He kept up a magnificent gloom until she left for the night. And then he danced a hornpipe of glee not with his legs, but in his heart. He had deliberately schemed to get rid of Mrs. Butt by means of Helen Rathbone. The idea had occurred to him as he entered the house. That was why he had encouraged her to talk freely about servants by assuring her that Mrs. Butt was not in the scullery, being well aware that Mrs. Butt was in the scullery. He had made a tool of the unsuspecting, good-natured Helen, smart though she was! He had transitory qualms of fear about the possible expensiveness of Helen. He had decidedly not meant that she should give up school and nearly thirty shillings a week. But, still, he had managed her so far, and he reckoned that he could continue to manage her.

He regretted that she had not praised his music. And Helen wrote the same evening to her mother. From a very long and very exciting letter the following excerpts may be culled:

'I saw the fat old servant in the scullery at once. But uncle thought she wasn't there. He is a funny old man rather silly, like most old men but I like him, and you can say what you please. He isn't silly really. I instantly decided that I would get rid of that servant. And I did do, and poor uncle never suspected. In a few days I shall come to live here. It's much safer. Supposing he was taken ill and died, and left all his money to hospitals and things, how awfully stupid that would be! I told him I should leave the school, and he didn't turn a hair. He's a dear, and I don't care a fig for his money except to spend it for him. His tiny house is simply lovely, terrifically clean, and in the loveliest order. But I've no intention that we shall stay here. I think I shall take a large house up at Hillport. Uncle is only old in some ways; in many ways he's quite young. So I hope he won't mind a change. By the way, he told me about your age. My dearest mother, how could you —' etc.

In such manner came Helen Rathbone to keep house for her great-stepuncle.

CHAPTER IX

A GREAT CHANGE

'Helen Rathbone,' said Uncle James one Tuesday afternoon, 'have ye been meddling in my cashbox?'

They were sitting in the front room, Helen in a light-grey costume that cascaded over her chair and half the next chair, and James Ollerenshaw in the déshabillé of his Turkish cap. James was at his desk. It is customary in the Five Towns, when you feel combative, astonished, or ironic towards another person, to address that other person by his full name.

'You left the key in your cashbox this morning, uncle' said Helen, glancing up from a book, 'while you were fiddling with your safe in your bedroom.'

He did not like the word 'fiddling.' It did not suit either his dignity or the dignity of his huge Milner safe.

'Well,' he said, 'and if did! I wasn't upstairs more nor five minutes, and th' new servant had na' come! There was but you and me in th' house.'

'Yes. But, you see, I was in a hurry to go out marketing, and I couldn't wait for you to come down.'

He ignored this remark. 'There's a ten-pun' note missing,' said he. 'Don't play them tricks on me, lass; I'm getting an oldish man. Where hast hidden it? I mun go to th' bank.' He spoke plaintively.

'My dear uncle,' she replied, 'I've not hidden your ten-pound note. I wanted some money in a hurry, so I took it. I've spent some of it.'

'Spent some of it!' he exclaimed. 'How much hast spent?'

'Oh, I don't know. But I make up my accounts every night.'

'Lass,' said he, staring firmly out of the window, 'this won't do. I let ye know at once. This wunna' do.' He was determined to be master in his own house. She also was determined to be master in his own house. Conflict was imminent.

'May I ask what you mean, uncle?'

He hesitated. He was not afraid of her. But he was afraid of her dress – not of the material, but of the cut of it. If she had been Susan in Susan's dowdy and wrinkled alpaca, he would have translated his just emotion into what critics call 'simple, nervous English' – that is to say, Shakespearean prose. But the aristocratic, insolent perfection of Helen's gown gave him pause.

'Why didn't you tell me?' he demanded.

'I merely didn't think of it,' said she. 'I've been very busy.'

'If you wanted money, why didn't you ask me for it?' he demanded.

'I've been here over a week,' said she, 'and you've given me a pound and a postal order for ten shillings, which I had to ask for. Surely you must have guessed uncle that even if I'd put the thirty shillings in the savings bank we couldn't live on the interest of it, and that I was bound to want more. Something like seventy meals have been served in this house since I entered it.'

'I gave Mrs. Butt a pound a wik,' he observed.

'But think what a good manager Mrs. Butt was!' she said, with the sweetness of a saint.

He was accustomed to distributing satire, but not to receiving it. And, receiving this snowball full in the mouth, he did not quite know what to do with it; whether to pretend that he had received nothing, or to call a policeman. He ended by spluttering.

'It's easy enough to ask for money when you want it,' he said.

'I hate asking for money,' she said. 'All women do.'

'Then am I to be inquiring every morning whether you want money?' he questioned, sarcastically.

'Certainly, uncle,' she answered. 'How else are you to know?'

Difficult to credit that that girl had been an angel of light all the week, existing in a paradise which she had created for herself, and for him! And now, to defend an action utterly indefensible, she was employing a tone that might be compared to some fiendish instrumental device of a dentist.

But James Ollerenshaw did not wish his teeth stopped, nor yet extracted. He had excellent teeth. And, in common with all men who have never taken thirty consecutive repasts alone with the same woman, he knew how to treat women, how to handle them, – the trout!

He stood up. He raised all his body. Helen raised only her eyebrows.

'Helen Rathbone!' Such was the exordium. As an exordium, it was faultless. But it was destined to remain a fragment. It goes down to history as a perfect fragment, like the beginning of a pagan temple that the death of gods has rendered superfluous.

For a dog-cart stopped in front of the house at that precise second, deposited a lady of commanding mien, and dashed off again. The lady opened James's gate and knocked at James's front door. She could not be a relative of a tenant. James was closely acquainted with all his tenants, and he had none of that calibre. Moreover, Helen had caused a small board to be affixed to the gate: 'Tenants will please go round to the back.'

'Bless us!' he murmured, angrily. And, by force of habit, he went and opened the door. Then he recognised the lady. It was Sarah Swetnam, eldest child of the large and tumultuously intellectual Swetnam family that lived in a largish house in a largish way higher up the road, and as to whose financial stability rumour always had something interesting to say.

'Is Miss Rathbone here?'

Before he could reply, there was an ecstatic cry behind him: 'Sally!' And another in front of him: 'Nell!'

In the very nick of time he slipped aside, and thus avoided the inconvenience of being crushed to pulp between two locomotives under full steam. It appeared that they had not met for some years, Sally having been in London. The reunion was an affecting sight, and such a sight as had never before been witnessed in James's house. The little room seemed to be full of fashionable women, to be all gloves, frills, hat, parasol, veil, and whirling flowers; also scent. They kissed, through Sally's veil first, and then she lifted the veil, and four vermilion lips clung together. Sally was even taller than Helen, with a solid waist; and older, more brazen. They both sat down. Fashionable women have a manner of sitting down quite different from that of ordinary women, such as the wives of James's tenants. They only touch the back of the chair at the top. They don't loll, but they only escape lolling by dint of gracefulness. It is an affair of curves, slants, descents, nicely calculated. They elaborately lead your eye downwards over gradually increasing expanses, and naturally you expect to see their feet – and you won't see their feet. The thing is apt to be disturbing to unhabituated beholders.

Then fashionable women always begin their conversation right off. There are no modest or shy or decently awkward silences at the start. They slip into a conversation as a duck into water. In three minutes Helen had told Sarah Swetnam everything about her leaving the school, and about her establishment with her great-stepuncle. And Sarah seemed delighted, and tapped the tiles of the floor with the tip of her sunshade, and gazed splendidly over the room.

'And there are your books there, I see!' she said, in her positive calm voice, pointing to a few hundred books that were stacked in a corner. 'How lovely! You remember you promised to lend me that book of Thoreau's – what did you call it? – and you never did!'

'Next time you come I'll find it for you,' said Helen.

Next time she came! This kind of visit would occur frequently, then! They were talking just as if James Ollerenshaw had been in Timbuctoo, instead of by the mantelpiece, when Sally suddenly turned to him.

'It must be very nice for you to have Nell like this!' She addressed him with a glowing smile.

They had never been introduced! A week ago they had passed each other in St. Luke's Square without a sign. Of the Swetnam family, James 'knew' the father alone, and him slightly. What chiefly impressed him in Sarah was her nerve. He said nothing; he was tongue-tied.

'It's a great change for you,' proceeded Sarah.

'Ay,' he agreed; 'it's that.'

CHAPTER X

A CALL

The next moment the two fluffy women had decided, without in the least consulting James, that they would ascend to Helen's bedroom to look at a hat which, James was surprised to learn, Helen had seen in Brunt's window that morning and had bought on the spot. No wonder she had been in a hurry to go marketing; no wonder she had spent 'some' of his ten-pound note! He had seen hats in Brunt's marked as high as two guineas; but he had not dreamt that such hats would ever enter his house. While he had been labouring, collecting his rents and arranging for repairs, throughout the length and the breadth of Bursley and Turnhill, she under pretence of marketing, had been flinging away ten-pound notes at Brunt's. The whole business was fantastic, simply and madly fantastic; so fantastic that he had not yet quite grasped the reality of it! The whole business was unheard of. He saw, with all the clearness of his masculine intellect, that it must cease. The force with which he decided within himself that it must cease – and instanter! – bordered upon the hysterical. As he had said, plaintively, he was an oldish man. His habits, his manners, and his notions, especially his notions about money, were fixed and set like plaster of Paris in a mould. Helen's conduct was nothing less than dangerous. It might bring him to a sudden death from heart disease. Happily, he had had a very good week indeed with his rents. He trotted about all day on Mondays and on Tuesday mornings, gathering his rents, and on Tuesday afternoons he usually experienced the assuaged content of an alligator after the weekly meal. Otherwise there was no knowing what might not have been the disastrous consequences of Helen's bare-faced robbery and of her unscrupulous, unrepentant defence of that robbery. For days and days he had imagined himself in heaven with a seraph

50

who was also a good cook. He had forty times congratulated himself on catching Helen. And now . . . !

But it must stop.

Then he thought of the cooking. His mouth remembered its first taste of the incomparable kidney omelette. What an ecstasy! Still, a ten-pound note for even a kidney omelette jarred on the fineness of his sense of values.

A feminine laugh – Helen's – came down the narrow stairs and through the kitchen. . . No, the whole house was altered, with well-bred, distinguished women's laughter floating about the stairs like that.

He called upon his lifelong friend and comforter – the concertina. That senseless thing of rosewood, ivory, ebony, mother-of-pearl, and leather, was to him what a brother, a pipe, a bull terrier, a trusted confidant, might have been to another James. And now, in the accents of the Hallelujah Chorus, it yielded to his squeezings the secret and sublime solace which men term poetry.

Then there was a second, and equally imperious, knock at the door.

He loosed his fingers from his friend, and opened the door.

Mr. Emanuel Prockter stood on the doorstep. Mr Emanuel Prockter wore a beautiful blue suit, with a white waistcoat and pale gold tie; yellow gloves, boots with pointed toes, a glossy bowler hat, a cane, and an eyeglass. He was an impeccable young man, and the avowed delight of his tailor, whose bills were paid by Mrs. Prockter.

'Is Miss Rathbone at home?' asked Emanuel, after a cough.

'Helen?'

'Ye-es.'

'Ay,' said James, grimly. 'Her's quite at home.'

'Can I see her?'

James opened more widely the door. 'Happen you'd better step inside,' said he.

'Thanks, Mr. Ollerenshaw. What – er – fine weather we're having!'

James ignored this quite courteous and truthful remark. He shut the door, went into the kitchen, and called up the stairs: 'Helen, a young man to see ye.'

In the bedroom, Helen and Sarah Swetnam had exhausted

the Brunt hat, and were spaciously at sea in an enchanted
ocean of miscellaneous gossip such as is only possible between
two highly educated women who scorn tittle-tattle. Helen had
the back bedroom; partly because the front bedroom was her
uncle's, but partly also because the back bedroom was just as
large as and much quieter than the other, and because she
preferred it. There had been no difficulty about furniture.
Even so good a landlord as James Ollerenshaw is obliged now
and then to go to extremes in the pursuit of arrears of rent, and
the upper part of the house was crowded with choice speci-
mens of furniture which had once belonged to the more
magnificent of his defaulting tenants. Helen's bedroom was
not 'finished'; nor, since she regarded it as a temporary
lodging rather than a permanent habitation, was she in a mind
to finish it. Still, with her frocks dotted about, the hat on the
four-post bed, and her silver-mounted brushes and manicure
tools on the dressing-table, it had a certain stylishness. Sarah
shared the bed with the hat. Helen knelt at a trunk.

'Whatever made you think of coming to Bursley?' Sarah
questioned.

'Don't you think it's better than Longshaw?' said Helen.

'Yes, my darling child. But that's not why you came. If you
ask me, I believe it was your deliberate intention to capture
your great-uncle. Anyhow, I congratulate you on your success.'

'Ah!' Helen murmured, smiling to herself, 'I'm not out of
the wood yet.'

'What do you mean?'

'Well, you see, uncle and I haven't quite decided whether he
is to have his way or I am to have mine; we were both
thinking about it when you happened to call.' And then, as
there was a little pause: 'Are people talking about us much?'

She did not care whether people were talking much or little,
but she had an obscure desire to shift ever so slightly the
direction of the conversation.

'I've only been here a day or two, so I can scarcely judge,'
said Sarah. 'But Lilian came in from the art school this
morning with an armful of chatter.'

'Let me see, I forget,' Helen said. 'Is Lilian the youngest, or
the next to the youngest?'

'My dearest child, Lilian is the youngest but one, of course; but she's grown up now – naturally.'

'What! When I saw her last, that day when she was with you at Knype, she had a ribbon in her hair, and she looked ten.'

'She's eighteen. And haven't you heard?'

'Heard what?'

'Do you mean to say you've been in Bursley a week and more, and haven't heard? Surely you know Andrew Dean?'

'I know Andrew Dean,' said Helen; and she said nothing else.

'When did you last see him?'

'Oh, about a fortnight ago.'

'It was before that. He didn't tell you? Well, it's just like him, that is; that's Andrew all over!'

'What is?'

'He's engaged to Lilian. It's the first engagement in the family, and she's the youngest but one.'

Helen shut the trunk with a snap, then opened it and shut it again. And then she rose, smoothing her hair.

'I scarcely know Lilian,' she said, coldly. 'And I don't know your mother at all. But I must call and congratulate the child. No, Andrew Dean didn't breathe a word.'

'I may tell you as a dreadful secret, Nell, that we aren't any of us in the seventh heaven about it. Aunt Annie said yesterday: "I don't know that I'm so set up with it as all that, Jane" (meaning mother). We aren't so set up with it as all that!'

'Why not?'

'Oh, we aren't. I don't know why. I pretend to be, lest Lilian should imagine I'm jealous.'

It was at this point that the voice of James Ollerenshaw announced a young man.

The remainder of that afternoon was like a bewildering dream to James Ollerenshaw. His front room seemed to be crowded with a multitude of peacocks, that would have been more at home under the sun of Mrs. Prockter's lawns up at Hillport. Yet there were only three persons present besides himself. But decidedly they were not of his world; they were of the world that referred to him as 'old Jimmy Ollerenshaw,' or briefly as 'Jimmy.' And he had to sit and listen to them, and even to answer coherently when spoken to. Emanuel Prockter was brilliant. He had put his hat on one chair and his cane across another, and he conversed with ducal facility. The two things about him that puzzled the master of the house were – first, why he was not, at such an hour, engaged in at any rate the pretence of earning his living; and, second, why he did not take his gloves off. No notion of work seemed to exist in the minds of the three. They chattered of tennis, novels, music, and particularly of amateur operatic societies. James acquired the information that Emanuel was famous as a singer of songs. The topic led them naturally to James's concertina, and then Emanuel swept it off to the afternoon tea-room of the new Midland Grand Hotel at Manchester, where Emanuel had lately been. And that led to the Old Oak Tree tea-house in Bond-street, where, not to be beaten by Emanuel, Sarah Swetnam had lately been.

'Suppose we have tea,' said Helen.

And she picked up a little brass bell which stood on the central table and tinkled it. James had not noticed the bell. It was one of the many little changes that Helen had introduced. Each change by itself was a nothing – what is one small bell in a house? – yet in the mass they amounted to much. The bell was obviously new. She must have bought it; but she had not mentioned it to him. And how could they all sit at the tiny table in the kitchen? Moreover, he had no fancy for entertaining the whole town of Bursley to meals. However, the immediate prospect of tea produced in James a feeling of satisfaction, even though he remained in perfect ignorance of the methods by which Helen meant to achieve the tea. She had rung the bell, and gone on talking, as if the tea would cook itself and walk in on its hind legs and ask to be eaten.

Then the new servant entered with a large tray. James had never seen such a servant, a servant so entirely new. She was wearing a black frock, and various parts of the frock, and the top of her head, were covered with stiffly-starched white linen – or was it cotton? Her apron, which had two pockets, was more elaborate than an antimacassar. Helen coolly instructed her to place the tray on his desk; which she did, brushing irreverently aside a number of rent books.

On the tray there was nothing whatever to eat but a dozen slices of the thinnest conceivable bread and butter.

Helen rose. Emanuel also rose.

Helen poured out the tea. Emanuel took a cup and saucer in one hand and the plate of bread and butter in the other, and ceremoniously approached Sarah Swetnam. Sarah accepted the cup and saucer, delicately chose a piece of bread and butter and lodged it on her saucer, and went on talking.

Emanuel returned to the table, and, reladen, approached old Jimmy, and old Jimmy had to lodge a piece of bread and butter on his saucer. Then Emanuel removed his gloves, and in a moment they were all drinking tea and nibbling bread and butter.

What a fall was this from kidney omelettes! And four had struck! Did Helen expect her uncle to make his tea off a slice of bread and butter that weighed about two drachms?

When the alleged tea was over James got on his feet, and silently slid into the kitchen. The fact was that Emanuel Prockter and the manikin airs of Emanuel Prockter made him positively sick. He had not been in the kitchen more than a minute before he was aware of amazing matters in the conversation.

'Yes,' said Helen; 'it's small.'

'But, my child, you've always been used to a small house, surely. I think it's just as quaint and pretty as a little museum.'

'Would you like to live in a little museum?'

A laugh from Emanuel, and the voice of Helen proceeding: 'I've always lived in a small house, just as I've taught six hours a day in a school. But not because I wanted to. I like room. I daresay that uncle and I may find another house one of these days.'

'Up at Hillport, I hope,' Emanuel put in. James could see his mincing imbecile smile through the kitchen wall.

'Who knows?' said Helen.

James returned to the front room. 'What's that ye're saying?' he questioned the company.

'I was just saying how quaint and pretty your house is,' said Sarah, and she rose to depart. More kissings, flutterings, swishings! Emanuel bowed.

Emanuel followed Miss Swetnam in a few minutes. Helen accompanied him to the gate, where she stayed a little while talking to him. James was in the blackest gloom.

'And now, you dear old thing,' said Helen, vivaciously bustling into the house, 'you shall have your *tea*. You've behaved like a perfect angel.'

And she kissed him on the cheek, very excitedly, as he thought. She gave him another kidney omelette for his tea. It was even more adorable than the former one. With the taste of it in his mouth, he could not recur to the question of the ten-pound note all at once. When tea was over she retired upstairs, and remained in retirement for ages. She descended at a quarter to eight, with her hat and gloves on. It appeared to him that her eyes were inflamed.

'I'm going out,' she said, with no further explanation.

And out she went, leaving the old man, stricken daft by too many sensations, to collect his wits.

He had not even been to the bank!

And the greatest sensation of all the night-marish days was still in reserve for him. At a quarter-past eight someone knocked at the door. He opened it being handier than the new servant. He imagined himself ready for anything; but he was not ready for the apparition which met him on the threshold.

Mrs. Prockter, of Hillport, asked to be admitted!

CHAPTER XI

ANOTHER CALL

Mrs. Procter was compelled to ask for admission, because James, struck moveless and speechless by the extraordinary sight of her, offered no invitation to enter. He merely stood in front of the half-opened door.

'May I come in, Mr. Ollerenshaw?' she said, very urbanely. 'I hope you will excuse this very informal call. I've altered my dinner hour in order to pay it.'

And she smiled. The smile seemed to rouse him from a spell.

'Come in, missis, do!' he conjured her, warmly.

He was James; he was even Jimmy; but he was also a man, very much a man, though the fact had only recently begun to impress itself on him. Mrs. Prockter, while a dowager – portly, possibly fussy, perhaps slightly comic to a younger generation – was still considerably younger than James. With her rich figure her excellent complexion, her carefully- cherished hair, and her apparel, she was a woman to captivate a man of sixty, whose practical experience of the sex extended over nine days.

'Thank you,' said she, gratefully.

He shut the front door, as if he were shutting a bird in a cage; and he also shut the door leading to the kitchen – a door which had not been shut since the kitchen fire smoked in the celebrated winter of 1897. She sat down at once in the easy-chair.

'Ah!' she exclaimed, in relief. And then she began to fan herself with a fan which was fastened to her person by a chain that might have moored a steamer.

James, searching about for something else to do while he was collecting his forces, drew the blind and lighted the gas. But it was not yet dark.

'I wonder what you will think of me, calling like this?' she said, with a sardonic smile.

It was apparent that, whatever he thought of her, she would not be disturbed or abashed. She was utterly at her ease. She could not, indeed, have recalled the moment when she had not been at her ease. She sat in the front room with all the external symptoms of being at home. This was what chiefly surprised James Ollerenshaw in his grand guests – they all took his front room for granted. They betrayed no emotion at its smallness or its plainness, or its eccentricities. He would somehow have expected them to signify, overtly or covertly, that that kind of room was not the kind of room to which they were accustomed.

'Anyhow, I'm glad to see ye, Mrs. Prockter,' James returned.

A speech which did not in the least startle Mrs. Prockter, who was thoroughly used to people being glad to see her. But it startled James. He had uttered it instinctively; it was the expression of an instinctive gladness which took hold of him and employed his tongue on its own account, and which rose superior even to his extreme astonishment at the visit. He *was* glad to see her. She was stout and magnificent, in her silk and her ribbons. He felt that he preferred stout women to thin; and that, without being aware of it, he had always preferred stout women to thin. It was a question of taste. He certainly preferred Mrs. Prockter to Sarah Swetnam. Mrs. Prockter's smile was the smile of a benevolently-cynical creature whose studies in human nature had reached the advanced stage. James was reassured by this, for it avoided the necessity for 'nonsense.' . . . Yes, she was decidedly better under a roof and a gas-jet than in the street.

'May I ask if your niece is in?' she said in a low voice.

'She isn't.'

He had been sure that she had called about Helen, if not to see Helen. But there was a conspiratorial accent in her question for which he was unprepared. So he sat down at last.

'Well,' said Mrs. Prockter, 'I'm not sorry she isn't. But if she had been I should have spoken just the same – not to her, but to you. Now, Mr. Ollerenshaw, I think you and I are rather alike in some things. I hate beating about the bush, and I imagine that you do.'

He was flattered. And he was perfectly eased by her tone. She was a woman to whom you could talk sense. And he perceived that, though a casual observer might fail to find the points of resemblance between them, they *were* rather alike.

'I expect,' said he, 'it's pretty well known i' this town as I'm not one that beats about the bush.'

'Good!' said she. 'You know my stepson, Emanuel?'

'He was here a bit since,' James replied.

'What do you think of him?'

'How?'

'As a man?'

'Well, missis, as we are na' beating about the bush, I think he's a foo'.'

'Now that's what I like!' she exclaimed, quite ravished. 'He *is* a fool, Mr. Ollerenshaw – between ourselves. I can see that you and I will get on together splendidly! Emanuel is a fool. I can't help it. I took him along with my second husband, and I do my best for him. But I'm not responsible for his character. As far as that goes, he isn't responsible for it, either. Not only is he a fool, but he is a conceited fool, and an idle fool; and he can't see a joke. At the same time he is quite honest, and I think he's a gentleman. But being a gentleman is no excuse for being a fool; indeed, I think it makes it worse.'

'Nothing can make it worse,' James put in.

She drew down the corners of her lips and stroked her fine grey hair.

'You say Emanuel has been here to-day?'

'Ay!' said James. 'He came in an' had a sup o' tea.'

'Do you know why he came?'

'Maybe he felt faintlike, and slipped in here, as there's no public nearer than the Queen Adelaide. Or maybe he thought as I was getting on in years, and he wanted for to make my acquaintance afore I died. I didna' ask him.'

'I see you understand,' said Mrs. Prockter. 'Mr. Ollerenshaw, my stepson is courting your niece.'

'Great-stepniece,' James corrected; and added: 'Is he now? To tell ye th' truth I didn't know till th'other day as they were acquainted.'

'They haven't been acquainted long,' Mrs. Prockter informed him. 'You may have heard that Emanuel is thinking of going into partnership with Mr. Andrew Dean – a new glaze that Mr. Dean has invented. The matter may turn out well, because all that Mr. Dean really wants is a sleeping partner with money. Emanuel has the money, and I think he can be guaranteed to sleep. Your stepniece met Emanuel by accident through Mr. Dean some weeks ago, over at Longshaw. They must have taken to each other at once. And I must tell you that not merely is my stepson courting your niece, but your niece is courting my stepson.'

'You surprise me, missis!'

'I daresay I do. But it is the fact. She isn't a Churchwoman; at least, she wasn't a Churchwoman at Longshaw; she was Congregational, and not very much at that. You aren't a Churchman, either; but your niece now goes to St. Luke's every Sunday. So does my stepson. Your niece is out to-night. So is my stepson. And if they are not together somewhere I shall be very much astonished. Of course, the new generation does as it likes.'

'And what next?' James inquired.

'I'll tell you what next,' cried the mature lady, with the most charming vivacity. 'I like your niece. I've met her twice at the St. Luke's Guild, and I like her. I should have asked her to come and see me, only I'm determined not to encourage her with Emanuel. Mr. Ollerenshaw, I'm not going to have her marrying Emanuel, and that's why I've come to see you.'

The horror of his complicated situation displayed itself suddenly to James. He who had always led a calm, unworried life, was about to be shoved into the very midst of a hullaballoo of women and fools.

His wizened body shrank; and he was not sure that his pride was quite unhurt. Mrs. Prockter noticed this.

'Oh!' she resumed, with undiminished vivacity, 'it's not because I think your niece isn't good enough for Emanuel; it's because I think she's a great deal too good! And yet it isn't that, either. The truth is, Mr. Ollerenshaw, I'm a purely selfish woman. I'm the last person in the world to stand in the way of my poor stepson getting a better wife than he deserves. And if the woman chooses to throw herself away on him, that's not my affair. What I scent danger in is that your stepniece would find my stepson out. At present she's smitten by his fancy waistcoat. But she would soon see through the fancy waistcoat – and then there would be a scandal. If I have not misjudged your stepniece, there would be a scandal, and I do not think that I have misjudged her. She is exactly the sort of young woman who, when she had discovered she had made a mistake, would walk straight out of the house.'

'She is!' James agreed with simple heartiness of conviction.

'And Emanuel, having no sense of humour, would leave nothing undone to force her back again. Imagine the scandal, Mr. Ollerenshaw! Imagine my position; imagine yours! Me, in an affair like that! I won't have it – that is to say, I won't have it if I can stop it. Now, what can we do?'

Despite the horror of the situation, he had sufficient loose, unemployed sentiment (left over from pitying himself) to be rather pleased by her manner of putting it: What can we do?

But he kept this pleasure to himself.

'Nowt!' he said, drily.

He spoke to her as one sensible person speaks to another sensible person in the Five Towns. Assuredly she was a very sensible person. He had in past years credited, or discredited, her with 'airs.' But here she was declaring that Helen was too good for her stepson. If his pride had momentarily suffered, through a misconception, it was now in the full vigour of its strength.

'You think we can do nothing?' she said, reflectively, and leant forward on her chair towards him, as if struck by his oracular wisdom.

'What can us do?'

'You might praise Emanuel to her – urge her on.' She fixed him with her eye.

Sensible? She was prodigious. She was the serpent of serpents.

He took her gaze twinkling. 'Ay!' he said. 'I might. But if I'm to urge her on, why didna' ye ask her to your house like, and chuck 'em at each other?'

She nodded several times, impressed by this argument. 'You are quite right, Mr. Ollerenshaw,' she admitted.

'It's a dangerous game,' he warned her.

She put her lips together in meditation, and stared into a corner.

'I must think it over' – she emerged from her reflections. 'I feel much easier now I've told you all about it. And I feel sure that two common-sense, middle-aged people like you and me can manage to do what we want. Dear me! How annoying stepsons are! Obviously, Emanuel ought to marry another fool. And goodness knows there are plenty to choose from. And yet he must needs go and fall in love with almost the only sensible girl in the town! There's no end to that boy's foolishness. He actually wants me to buy Wilbraham Hall, furniture, and everything! What do you think it's worth, Mr. Ollerenshaw?'

'Worth? It's worth what it'll fetch.'

'Eight thousand?'

'Th' land's worth that,' said James.

'It's a silly idea. But he put it into my head. Now will you drop in one day and see me?'

'No,' said James. 'I'm not much for tea-parties, thank ye.'

'I mean when I'm alone,' she pleaded, delightfully; 'so that we can talk over things, and you can tell me what is going on.'

He saw clearly all the perils of such a course, but his instinct seized him again.

'Happen I may look in some morning when I'm round yonder.'

'That will be very nice of you,' she flattered him, and rose.

Helen came home about ten o'clock, and went direct to bed. Never before had James Ollerenshaw felt like a criminal, but as Helen's eyes dwelt for a moment on his in bidding him good-night, he could scarcely restrain the blush of the evil-doer. And him sixty! Turn which way he would he saw nothing but worry. What an incredible day he had lived through! And how astounding was human existence!

CHAPTER XII

BREAKFAST

He had an unsatisfactory night – that is to say, in the matter of sleep. In respect of sagacity he rose richer than he had lain down. He had clearly perceived, about three a.m., that he was moving too much in circles which were foreign to him, and which called him 'Jimmy.' And at five a.m., when the first workmen's car woke bumpily the echoes of the morn, he had perceived that Mrs. Prockter's plan for separating Emanuel and Helen by bringing them together was not a wise plan. Of course, Helen must not marry Emanuel Prockter. The notion of such a union was ludicrous. (In spite of all the worry she was heaping upon him, he did not see any urgent reason why she should marry anybody). But the proper method of nipping the orange-blossom in the bud was certainly to have a plain chat with Helen, one of those plain chats which can only occur, successfully, between plain, commonsense persons. He was convinced that, notwithstanding Mrs. Prockter's fears, Helen had not for an instant thought of Emanuel as a husband. It was inconceivable that she, a girl so utterly sensible, should have done so. And yet – girls! And Mrs. Prockter was no fool, come to think of it. A sterling creature. Not of his world but nevertheless – At this point he uneasily dozed.

However, he determined to talk with Helen that morning at breakfast. He descended at half-past seven, as usual, full of a diplomatic intention to talk to Helen. She was wholly sensible; she was a person to whom you *could* talk. Still, tact would be needed. Lack of sleep had rendered his nervous system such that he would have preferred to receive tact rather than to give it. But, happily, he was a self-controlled man.

His post, which lay scattered on the tiles at the foot of the front door, did not interest him. He put it aside, in its basket. Nor could he work, according to his custom, at his accounts.

Even the sight of the unfilled-in credit-slips for the bank did not spur him to industry. There can be no doubt that he was upset.

He walked across the room to the piles of Helen's books against the wall, and in sheer absence of mind picked one up, and sat on a chair, on which he had never before sat, and began to read the volume.

Then the hurried, pretentious striking of the kitchen clock startled him. Half-an-hour had passed in a moment. He peeped into the kitchen. Not a sign of breakfast! Not a sign of the new servant, with her starched frills! And for thirty years he had breakfasted at eight o'clock precisely.

And no Helen! Was Helen laughing at him? Was Helen treating him as an individual of no importance? It was unimaginable that his breakfast should be late. If anybody thought that he was going to – No! he must not give way to righteous resentment. Diplomacy! Tact! Forbearance!

But he would just go up to Helen's room and rap, and tell her of the amazing and awful state of things on the ground-floor. As a fact, she herself was late. At that moment she appeared.

'Good-morning, uncle.'

She was cold, prim, cut off like China from human intercourse by a wall.

'Th' servant has na' come,' said he, straining to be tolerant and amicable. He did his best to keep a grieved astonishment out of his voice; but he could not.

'Oh!' she murmured, calmly. It was nothing to her, then, that James's life should be turned upside down! And she added, with icy detachment: 'I'm not surprised. You'll never get servants to be prompt in the morning when they don't sleep in the house. And there's no room for Georgiana to sleep in the house.'

Georgiana! Preposterous name!

'Mrs. Butt was always prompt. I'll say that for her,' he replied.

This, as he immediately recognised, was a failure in tact on his part. So when she said quickly: 'I'm sure Mrs. Butt would be delighted to come back if you asked her,' he said nothing.

What staggered his intellect and his knowledge of human nature was that she remained absolutely unmoved by this appalling, unprecedented, and complete absence of any sign of breakfast at after eight o'clock.

Just then Georgiana came. She had a key to the back door, and entered the house by way of the scullery.

'Good morning Georgiana,' Helen greeted her, going into the scullery – much more kindly than she had greeted her uncle. Instead of falling on Georgiana and slaying her, she practically embraced her.

A gas cooking-stove is a wondrous gift of Heaven. You do not have to light it with yesterday's paper, damp wood, and the remains of last night's fire. In twelve minutes not merely was the breakfast ready, but the kitchen was dusted, and there was a rose in a glass next to the bacon. James had calmed himself by reading the book, and the period of waiting had really been very short. As he fronted the bacon and the flower, Helen carefully shut the scullery door. The *Manchester Guardian* lay to the left of his plate. Thoughtful! Altogether it was not so bad.

Further, she smiled in handing him his tea. She, too, he observed, must have slept ill. Her agreeable face was drawn. But her blue-and-white-striped dress was impeccably put on. It was severe, and yet very smooth. It suited her mood. It also suited his. They faced each other, as self-controlled people do face each other at breakfast after white nights, disillusioned, tremendously sensible, wise, gently cynical, seeing the world with steady and just orbs.

'I've been reading one o' your books, lass,' he began, with superb amiability. 'It's pretty near as good as a newspaper. There's summat about a law case as goes on for ever. It isna' true, I suppose, but it might be. The man as wrote that knew what he was talking about for once in a way. It's rare and good.'

'You mean Jarndyce v. Jarndyce?' she said, with a smile – not one of her condescending smiles.

'Ay,' he said, 'I believe that *is* the name. How didst know, lass?'

'I just guessed,' she answered. 'I suppose you don't have much time for reading, uncle?'

'Not me!' said he. 'I'm one o' th' busiest men in Bosley. And if ye don't know it now, you will afore long.'

'Oh!' she cried, 'I've noticed that. But what can you expect? With all those rents to collect yourself! Of course, I think you're quite right to collect them yourself. Rent-collectors can soon ruin a property.' Her tone was exceedingly sympathetic and comprehending. He was both surprised and pleased by it. He had misjudged her mood. It was certainly comfortable to have a young woman in the house who understood things as she did.

'Ye're right, lass,' he said. 'It's small houses as mean trouble. You're never done – wi' cottage property. Always summat!'

'It's all small, isn't it?' she went on. 'About how much do the rents average? Three-and-six a week?'

'About that,' he said. She was a shrewd guesser.

'I can't imagine how you carry the money about,' she exclaimed. 'It must be very heavy for you.'

'I'll tell you,' he explained. 'I've got my own system o' collecting. If I hadn't, I couldna' get through. In each street I've one tenant as I trust. And the other tenants can leave their rent and their rent books there. When they do that regular for a month, I give 'em twopence apiece for their children. If they do it regular for a year, I mak' 'em a present of a wik's rent at Christmas. It's cheaper nor rent-collectors.'

'What a good idea!' she said, impressed. 'But how *do* you carry the money about?'

'I bank i' Bosley, and I bank i' Turnhill, too. And I bank once i' Bosley and twice i' Turnhill o' Mondays, and twice i' Bosley o' Tuesdays. Only yesterday I was behind. I reckon as I can do all my collecting between nine o'clock Monday and noon Tuesday. I go to the worst tenants first – be sure o' that. There's some o' 'em, if you don't catch 'em early o' Monday, you don't catch 'em at all.'

'It's incredible to me how you can do it all in a day and a half,' she pursued. 'Why, how many houses are there?'

'Near two hundred and forty i' Bosley,' he responded. 'Hast forgotten th' sugar this time, lass?'

'And in Turnhill?' she said, passing the sugar. 'I think I'll have that piece of bacon if you don't want it.'

'Over a hundred,' said he. 'A hundred and twenty.'

'So that, first and last, you have to handle about sixty

pounds each week, and all in silver and copper. Fancy! What a weight it must be!'

'Ay!' he said, but with less enthusiasm.

'That's three thousand a-year,' she continued.

Her tone was still innocuously sympathetic. She seemed to be talking of money as she might have talked of counters. Nevertheless, he felt that he had been entrapped.

'I expect you must have saved at the very least thirty thousand pounds by this time,' she reflected, judicially, disinterestedly – speaking as a lawyer might have spoken.

He offered no remark.

'That means another thirty pounds a week,' she resumed. Decidedly she was marvellous at sums of interest.

He persisted in offering no remark.

'By the way,' she said, 'I must look into my household accounts. How much did you tell me you allowed Mrs. Butt a week for expenses?'

'A pound,' he replied, shortly.

She made no comment. 'You don't own the house, do you?' she inquired.

'No,' he said.

'What's the rent?'

'Eighteen pounds,' he said. Reluctant is a word that inadequately described his attitude.

'The worst of this house is that it has no bathroom,' she remarked. 'Still, eighteen pounds a year is eighteen pounds a year.'

Her tone was faultless, in its innocent, sympathetic common sense. The truth was, it was too faultless; it rendered James furious with a fury that was dangerous, because it had to be suppressed.

Then suddenly she left the table.

'The Kiel butter at a shilling a pound is quite good enough, Georgiana,' he heard her exhorting the servant in the scullery.

Ten minutes later, she put ten sovereigns in front of him.

'There's that ten-pound note,' she said, politely (but not quite accurately). 'I've got enough of my own to get on with.'

She fled ere he could reply.

And not a word had he contrived to say to her concerning Emanuel.

CHAPTER XIII

THE WORLD

A few days later James Ollerenshaw was alone in the front room, checking various accounts for repairs of property in Turnhill, when twin letters fell into the quietude of the apartment. The postman – the famous old postman of Bursley, who on fine summer days surmounted the acute difficulty of tender feet by delivering mails in worsted slippers – had swiftly pushed the letters, as usual, through the slit in the door; but, nevertheless, their advent had somehow the air of magic, as, indeed, the advent of letters always had. Mr. Ollerenshaw glanced curiously from his chair, over his spectacles, at the letters as they lay dead on the floor. Their singular appearance caused him to rise at once and pick them up. They were sealed with a green seal, and addressed in a large and haughty hand – one to Helen and the other to himself. Obviously they came from the world which referred to him as 'Jimmy.' He was not used to being thrilled by mere envelopes, but now he became conscious of a slight quickening of pulsation. He opened his own envelope – the paper was more like a blanket than paper, and might have been made from the material of a child's untearable picture-book. He had to use a stout paper-knife, and when he did get into the envelope he felt like a burglar.

The discerning and shrewd ancient had guessed the contents. He had feared, and he had also hoped, that the contents would comprise an invitation to Mrs. Prockter's house at Hillport. They did; and more than that. The signature was Mrs. Prockter's, and she had written him a four-page letter. 'My dear Mr. Ollerenshaw,' 'Believe me, yours most cordially and sincerely, Flora Prockter.'

Flora!

The strangest thing, perhaps, in all this strange history is that he thought the name suited her.

He had no intention of accepting the invitation. Not exactly! But he enjoyed receiving it. It constituted a unique event in his career. And the wording of it was very agreeable. Mrs. Prockter proceeded thus: 'In pursuance of our plan' – our plan! – 'I am also inviting your niece. Indeed, I have gathered from Emanuel that he considers her as the prime justification of the party. We will throw them together. She will hear him sing. She has never heard him sing. If this does not cure her, nothing will, though he has a nice voice. I hope it will be a fine night, so that we may take the garden. I did not thank you half enough for the exceedingly kind way in which you received my really unpardonable visit the other evening,' etc.

James had once heard Emanuel Prockter sing, at a concert given in aid of something which deserved every discourage-ment, and he agreed with Mrs. Prockter; not that he pretended to know anything about singing.

He sat down again, to compose a refusal to the invitation; but before he had written more than a few words it had transformed itself into an acceptance. He was aware of the entire ridiculous-ness of his going to an evening party at Mrs. Prockter's; still, an instinct, powerful but obscure (it was the will-to-live, and naught else), persuaded him by force to say that he would go.

'Have you had an invitation from Mrs. Prockter?' Helen asked him at tea.

'Yes,' said he. 'Have you?'

'Yes,' said she. 'Shall you go?'

'Ay, lass, I shall go.'

She seemed greatly surprised. 'Us'll go together,' he said.

'I don't think that I shall go,' said she, hesitatingly.

'Have ye written to refuse?'

'No.'

'Then I should advise ye to go, my lass.'

'Why?'

'Unless ye want to have trouble with me,' said he, grimly.

'But, uncle —'

'It's no good butting uncle,' he replied. 'If ye did na' mean to go, why did ye give young Prockter to understand as ye would go? I'll tell ye why ye changed your mind, lass. It's because you're ashamed o' being seen there with yer old uncle, and I'm sorry for it.'

'Uncle!' she protested. 'How can you say such a thing? You ought to know that no such idea ever entered my head.'

He did know that no such idea had ever entered her head, and he was secretly puzzling for the real reason of her projected refusal. But, being determined that she should go, he had employed the surest and the least scrupulous means of achieving his end.

He tapped nervously on the table, and maintained the silence of the wounded and the proud.

'Of course, if you take it in that way,' she said, after a pause, 'I will go.'

And he went through the comedy of gradually recovering from a wound.

His boldness in accepting the invitation and in compelling Helen to accompany him was the audacity of sheer ignorance. He had not surmised the experiences which lay before him. She told him to order a cab. She did not suggest the advisability of a cab. She stated, as a platitude, the absolute indispensability of a cab. He had meant to ride to Hillport in the tramcar, which ran past Mrs. Prockter's gate. However, he relqvtwntly agrezbhto order a cab, being fearful lest she might, after all, refuse to go. It was remarkable that, after having been opposed to the policy of throwing Helen and Emanuel together, he was now in favour of it.

On the evening, when at five minutes past nine she came into the front room clad for Mrs Prockter's party, he perceived that the tramcar would have been unsuitable. A cab might hold her. A hansom would certainly not have held her. She was all in white, and very complicated. No hat; simply a white, silver-spangled bandage round her head, neck and shoulders!

She glanced at him. He wore his best black clothes. 'You look very well,' said she, surprisingly. 'That old-fashioned black necktie is splendid.'

So they went. James had the peculiar illusion that he was going to a belated funeral, for except at funerals he had never in his life ridden in a cab.

When he descended with his fragile charge in Mrs. Prockter's illuminated porch, another cab was just ploughing up the gravel of the drive in departure, and nearly the whole tribe of

Swetnams was on the doorstep; some had walked, and were boasting of speed. There were Sarah Swetnam, her brother Ted, the lawyer, her brother Ronald, the borough surveyor, her brother Adams, the bank cashier, and her sister Enid, aged seventeen. This child was always called 'Jos' by the family, because they hated the same 'Enid,' which they considered to be 'silly.' Lilian, the newly-affianced one, was not in the crowd.

'Where's Lilian?' Helen asked abruptly.

'Oh, she came earlier with the powerful Andrew,' replied the youthful and rather jealous Jos. 'She isn't an ordinary girl now.'

Sarah rapidly introduced her brothers and sister to James. They were all very respectful and agreeable; and Adams Swetnam pressed his hand quite sympathetically, and Jos's frank smile was delicious. What surprised him was that nobody seemed surprised at his being there. None of the girls wore hats, he noticed, and he also noticed that the three men (all about thirty in years) wore silk hats, white mufflers, and blue overcoats.

A servant – a sort of special edition of James's Georgiana – appeared, and robbed everybody of every garment that would yield easily to pulling. And then those lovely creatures stood revealed. Yes, Sarah herself was lovely under the rosy shades. The young men were elegantly slim, and looked very much alike, except that Adams had a beard – a feeble beard, but a beard. It is true that in their exact correctness they might have been mistaken for toast-masters, or, with the slight addition of silver neck-chains, for high officials in a costly restaurant. But great-stepuncle James could never have been mistaken for anything but a chip of the early nineteenth century flicked by the hammer of Fate into the twentieth. His wide black neck-tie was the secret envy of the Swetnam boys.

The Swetnam boys had the air of doing now what they did every night of their lives. With facile ease, they led the way through the long hall to the drawing-room. James followed, and *en route* he observed at the extremity of a side-hall two young people sitting with their hands together in a dusky corner. 'Male and female created He them!'

reflected James, with all the tolerant, disdainful wisdom of his years and situation.

A piano was then heard, and as Ronald Swetnam pushed open the drawing-room door for the women to enter, there came the sound of a shocked 'S-sh!'

Whereupon the invaders took to the tips of their toes and crept in as sinners. At the farther end a girl was sitting at a grand piano, and in front of the piano, glorious, effulgent, monarchical, stood Emanuel Prockter, holding a piece of music horizontally at the level of his waist. He had a white flower in his buttonhole, and, adhering to a quaint old custom which still lingers in the Five Towns, and possibly elsewhere, he showed a crimson silk handkerchief tucked in between his shirt-front and his white waistcoat. He had broad bands down the sides of his trousers. Not a hair of his head had been touched by the accidental winds of circumstance. He surveyed the couple of dozen people in the large, glowing room with a fixed smile and gesture of benevolent congratulation.

Mrs. Prockter was close to the door. 'Emanuel is just going to sing,' she whispered, and shook hands silently with James Ollerenshaw first.

CHAPTER XIV

SONG, SCENE AND DANCE

Every head was turned. Emanuel coughed, frowned, and put his left hand between his collar and his neck, as though he had concealed something there. The new arrivals slipped cautiously into chairs. James was between Helen and Jos. And he distinctly saw Jos wink at Helen, and Helen wink back. The winks were without doubt an expression of sentiments aroused by the solemnity of Emanuel's frown.

The piano tinkled on, and then Emanuel's face was observed to change. The frown vanished, and a smile of heavenly rapture took its place. His mouth gradually opened till its resemblance to the penultimate vowel was quite realistic, and simultaneously, by a curious muscular co-ordination, he rose on his toes to a considerable height in the air.

The strain was terrible, – like waiting for a gun to go off. James was conscious of a strange vibration by his side, and saw that Jos Swetnam had got the whole of a lace handkerchief into her mouth.

The gun went off – not with a loud report, but with a gentle and lofty tenor piping, somewhere in the neighbourhood of F, or it might have been only E (though, indeed, a photograph would have suggested that Emanuel was singing at lowest the upper C), and the performer slowly resumed his normal stature.

'O Love!' he had exclaimed, adagio and sostenuto.

Then the piano, in its fashion, also said: 'O Love!'

'O Love!' Emanuel exclaimed again, with slight traces of excitement, and rising to heights of stature hitherto undreamt of.

And the piano once more, in turn, called plaintively on love.

It would be too easy to mock Emanuel's gift of song. I leave that to people named Swetnam. There can be no doubt

73

Emanuel had a very taking voice, if thin, and that his singing gave pleasure to the majority of his hearers. More than any one else, it pleased himself. When he sang he seemed to be inspired by the fact, to him patent, that he was conferring on mankind a boon inconceivably precious. If he looked a fool, his looks seriously misinterpreted his feelings. He did not spare himself on that evening. He told his stepmother's guests all about love and all about his own yearnings. He hid nothing from them. He made no secret of the fact that he lived for love alone, that he had known innumerable loves, but none like one particular variety, which he described in full detail. As a confession, and especially as a confession uttered before many maidens, it did not err on the side of reticence. Presently, having described a kind of amorous circle, he came again to: 'O Love!'

But this time his voice cracked: which made him angry, with a stern and controlled anger. Still singing, he turned slowly to the pianist, and fiercely glared at the pianist's unconscious back. The obvious inference was that if his voice had cracked the fault was the pianist's. The pianist, poor thing, utterly unaware of the castigation she was receiving, stuck to her business. Less than a minute later, Emanuel's voice cracked again. This time he turned even more deliberately to the pianist. He was pained. He stared during five complete bars at the back of the pianist, still continuing his confession. He wished the audience to understand clearly where the blame lay. Finally, when he thought the pianist's back was sufficiently cooked, he faced the audience.

'I hope the pianist will not be so atrociously clumsy as to let my voice crack again,' he seemed to be saying.

Evidently his reproof to the pianist's back was effectual, for his voice did not crack again.

And at length, when Jos had communicated her vibration to all her family, and everyone had ceased to believe that the confession would ever end, the confession did end . It ended as it had begun, in an even, agreeable tenor piping. Emanuel was much too great an artist to allow himself to be carried away by his emotion. The concluding words were, 'Oh, rapture!' and Emanuel sang them just as if he had been singing 'One-and-eleven-pence three-farthings.'

'Oh, rats!' said Jos, under cover of the impassioned applause.

'It was nearly as long as Jarndyce v. Jarndyce,' observed Adams, under the same cover.

'What!' cried James, enchanted. 'Have you been reading that too?'

Adams Swetnam and great-step-uncle James had quite a little chat on the subject of Jarndyce v. Jarndyce. Several other people, including the hostess, joined in the conversation, and James was surprised at the renown which Jarndyce v. Jarndyce seemed to enjoy; he was glad to find his view shared on every hand. He was also glad, and startled, to discover himself a personality in the regions of Hillport. He went through more formal introductions in ten minutes than he had been through during the whole of his previous life. It was a hot evening; he wiped his brow. Then iced champagne was served to him. Having fluttered round him, in her ample way, and charmingly flattered him, Mrs. Prockter left him, encircled chiefly by young women, in order to convey to later arrivals that they, and they alone, were the authentic objects of her solicitude. Emanuel Prockter, clad in triumph, approached, and questioned James, as one shrewd man of business may question another, concerning the value in the market of Wilbraham Hall.

Shortly afterwards, a remarkable occurrence added zest to the party. Helen had wandered away with Sarah and Jos Swetnam. She re-entered the drawing-room while James and Emanuel were in discussion, and her attitude towards Emanuel was decidedly not sympathetic. Then Sarah Swetnam came in alone. And then Andrew Dean came in alone.

'Oh, here's Andrew, Helen!' Sarah exclaimed.

Andrew Dean had the air of a formidable personage. He was a tall, heavy, dark young man, with immense sloping shoulders, a black moustache, and incandescent eyes, which he used as though he were somewhat suspicious of the world in general. If his dress had been less untidy, he would have made a perfect villain of melodrama. He smiled the unsure smile of a villain as he awkwardly advanced, with outstretched hand, to Helen.

Helen put her lips together, kept her hands well out of view, and offered him a bow that could only have been properly appreciated under a microscope.

The episode was quite negative; but it amounted to a scene – a scene at one of Mrs. Prockter's parties! A scene, more-over, that mystified everybody; a scene that implied war and the wounded!

Some discreetly withdrew. Of these was Emanuel, who had the sensitiveness of an artist.

Andrew Dean presently perceived, after standing for some seconds like an imbecile stork on one leg, that the discretion of the others was worthy to be imitated. At the door he met Lilian, and they disappeared together arm in arm, as betrothed lovers should. Three people remained in that quarter of the drawing-room – Helen, her uncle, and Sarah Swetnam.

'Why, Nell,' said Sarah, aghast, 'what's the matter?'

'Nothing,' said Helen, calmly.

'But surely you shake hands with Andrew when you meet him, don't you?'

'That depends how I feel, my dear,' said Helen.

'Then something *is* the matter?'

'If you want to know,' said Helen, with haughtiness, 'in the hall, just now – that is – I – I overheard Mr. Dean say something about Emanuel Prockter's singing which I consider very improper.'

'But we all —'

'I'm going out into the garden,' said Helen.

'A pretty how-d'ye-do!' James muttered inaudibly to himself as he meandered to and from in the hall, observing the manners and customs of Hillport society. Another couple were now occupying the privacy of the seat at the end of the side-hall, and James noticed that the heads of this couple had precisely the same relative positions as the heads of the previous couple. 'Bless us!' he murmured, apropos of the couple, who, seeing in him a spy, rose and fled. Then he resumed his silent soliloquy. 'A pretty how-d'ye-do! The chit's as fixed on that there Emanuel Prockter as ever a chit could be!' And yet James had caught the winking with Jos Swetnam during the song! As an enigma, Helen grew darker and darker to him. He was almost ready to forswear his former belief, and to assert positively that Helen had no sense whatever.

Mrs. Prockter loomed up, disengaged. 'Ah, Mr. Ollerenshaw,' she said, 'everybody seems to be choosing the garden. Shall we go there? This way.'

She led him down the side-hall. 'By the bye,' she murmured, with a smile, 'I think our plan is succeeding.'

And, without warning him, she sat down in the seat, and of course he joined her, and she put her head close to his, evidently in a confidential mood.

'Bless us! he said to himself, apropos of himself and Mrs. Prockter, glancing about for spies.

'It's horrid of me to make fun of poor dear Emanuel's singing,' pursued Mrs. Prockter. 'But how did she take it? If I am not mistaken, she winked.'

'Her winked,' said James; 'yes, her winked.'

'Then everything's all right.'

'Missis' said he, 'if you don't mind what ye're about, you'll have a daughter-in-law afore you can say "knife"!'

'Not Helen?'

'Ay, Helen.'

'But, Mr. Ollerenshaw —'

Here happened an interruption – a servant with a tray of sustenance, comprising more champagne. James, prudent, would have refused, but under the hospitable urgency of Mrs. Prockter he compromised – and yielded.

'I'll join ye.'

So she joined him. Then a string of young people passed the end of the side-hall, and among them was Jos Swetnam, who capered up to the old couple on her long legs.

'Oh, Mrs. Prockter,' she cried, 'what a pity we can't dance on the lawn!'

'I wish you could, my dear,' said Mrs Prockter.

'And why can't ye?' demanded James.

'No music!' said Jos.

'You see,' Mrs. Prockter explained, 'the lawn is at the far end of the garden, and it is impossible to hear the piano so far off. If it were only a little piano we could move it about, but it's a grand piano.'

In James's next speech was to be felt the influence of champagne. 'Look here,' he said, 'it's nobbut a step from here to the Green Man, is it?'

'The Green Man!' echoed Mrs. Prockter, not comprehending.

'Ay, the pub!'

'I believe there is an inn at the bend,' said Mrs. Prockter; 'but I don't think I've ever noticed the sign.'

'It's the Green Man,' said James. 'If you'll send someone round there, and the respex of Mr. Ollerenshaw to Mr. Benskin – that's the landlord – and will he lend me the concertina as I sold him last Martinmas?'

'Oh, Mr. Ollerenshaw!' shrieked Jos. 'Can you play for dancing? How perfectly lovely it would be!'

'I fancy as I can keep *your* trotters moving, child,' said he, gaily.

Upon this, two spinsters, the Misses Webber, wearing duplicates of one anxious visage, supervened, and, with strange magic gestures, beckoned Mrs. Prockter away. News of the episode between Andrew Dean and Helen had at length reached them, and they had deemed it a sacred duty to inform the hostess of the sad event. They were of the species of woman that spares neither herself nor others. Their fault was, that they were too compassionate for this world. Promising to send the message to Mr. Benskin, Mrs. Prockter vanished to her doom.

Within a quarter of an hour a fête unique in the annals of Hillport had organised itself on the lawn in the dim, verdurous retreats behind Mrs. Prockter's house. The lawn was large enough to be just too small for a tennis-court. It was also of a pretty mid-Victorian irregularity as regards shape, and guarded from the grim horizons of the Five Towns by a ring of superb elms. A dozen couples, mainly youngish, promenaded upon its impeccable surface in obvious expectation; while on the borders, in rustic chairs, odd remnants of humanity, mainly oldish, gazed in ecstasy at the picturesque ensemble. In the midst of the lawn was Mrs. Prockter's famous weeping willow, on whose branches Chinese lanterns had been hung by a reluctant gardener, who held to the proper gardener's axiom that lawns are made to be seen and not hurt. The moon aided these lanterns to the best of her power. Under the tree was a cane chair, and on the cane chair sat an ageing man with a concertina between his hands. He put his head on one side and played a few bars, and the couples posed themselves expectantly. 'Hold on a bit!' the virtuoso called out. 'It's a tidy bit draughty here.'

He put the concertina on his knees, fumbled in his tail-pocket, and drew forth a tasselled Turkish cap, which majestically he assumed; the tassel fell over his forehead. He owned several Turkish caps, and never went abroad without one.

Then he struck up definitely, and Mrs. Prockter's party had resolved itself, as parties often do, into a dance. In the blissful excitation caused by the ancient and jiggy tunes which 'Jimmy' played, the sad episode of Helen Rathbone and Andrew Dean appeared to be forgotten. Helen danced with every man except Andrew, and Andrew danced with every woman except Helen. But Mrs. Prockter had not forgotten the episode; nor had the Misses Webber. The reputation of Mrs. Prockter's entertainments for utter correctness, and her own enormous reputation for fine tact, were impaired, and Mrs. Prockter was determined that that which ought to happen should happen.

She had a brief and exceedingly banal interview with Helen, and another with Andrew. And an interval having elapsed, Andrew was observed to approach Helen and ask her for a polka. Helen punctiliously accepted. And he led her out. The outraged gods of social decorum were appeased, and the reputations of Mrs. Prockter and her parties stood as high as ever. It was well and diplomatically done.

Nevertheless, the unforeseen came to pass. For at the end of the polka Helen fainted on the grass; and not Andrew but Emanuel was first to succour her. It was a highly-disconcerting climax. Of course, Helen, being Helen, recovered with singular rapidity. But that did not lighten the mystery.

In the cab, going home, she wept. James could scarcely have believed it of her.

'Oh, uncle,' she half whispered, in a voice of grief, 'you fiddled while Rome was burning!'

This obscure saying baffled him, the more so that he had been playing a concertina and not a fiddle at all. His feelings were vague, and in some respects contradictory; but he was convinced that Mrs. Prockter's scheme for separating Helen and the Apollo Emanuel was not precisely succeeding.

CHAPTER XV

THE GIFT

After that night great-step-uncle James became more than a celebrity – he became a notoriety in Bursley. Had it not been for the personal influence of Mrs. Prockter with the editor of the *Signal*, James's exploits upon the concertina under weeping willows at midnight would have received facetious comment in the weekly column of gossip that appears in the great daily organ of the Five Towns on Saturdays. James, aided by nothing but a glass or two of champagne, had suddenly stepped into the forefront of the town's life. He was a card. He rather liked being a card.

But within his own heart the triumph and glory of James Ollerenshaw were less splendid than outside it. Helen, apparently ashamed of having wept in his waistcoat, kept him off with a kind of a rod of stiff politeness. He could not get near her, and for at least two reasons he was anxious to get near her. He wanted to have that frank, confidential talk with her about the general imbecility of her adorer, Emanuel Prockter – that talk which he had failed to begin on the morning when she had been so sympathetic concerning his difficulties in collecting a large income. Her movements from day to day were mysterious. Facts pointed to the probability that she and Emanuel were seeing each other with no undue publicity. And yet, despite facts, despite her behaviour at the party, he could scarcely believe that shrewd Helen had not pierced the skin of Emanuel and perceived the emptiness therein. At any rate, Emanuel had not repeated his visit to the house. The only visitors had been Sarah Swetnam and her sister Lilian, the fiancée of Andrew Dean. The chatter of the three girls had struck James as being almost hysterically gay. But in the evening Helen was very gloomy, and he fancied a certain redness in her eyes. Though Helen was assuredly the last woman in the world to cry, she had, beyond doubt, cried once, and he now suspected her of another weeping.

Even more detrimental to his triumph in his own heart was the affair of the ten-pound note, which she had stolen (or abstracted if you will) and then restored to him with such dramatic haughtiness. That ten pounds was an awful trial to him. It rankled, not only with him, but (he felt sure) with her. Still, if she had her pride, he also had his. He reckoned that she had not rightly behaved in taking the note without his permission, and that in returning the full sum, and pretending that he had made it necessary for her to run the house on her own money, she had treated him meanly. The truth was, she had wounded him – again. Instincts of astounding generosity were budding in him, but he was determined to await an advance from her. He gave her money for housekeeping, within moderation, and nothing more.

Then one evening she announced that the morrow would be her birthday. James felt uneasy. He had never given birthday presents, but he well knew that presents were the correct thing on birthdays. He went to bed in a state of the most absurd and causeless mental disturbance. He did not know what to do. Whereas it was enormously obvious what to do.

He woke up about one o'clock, and reflected, with an air of discovery: 'Her tone was extremely friendly when she told me it was her birthday tomorrow. She meant it as an advance. I shall take it as an advance.'

About half-past one he said to himself; 'I'll give her a guinea to spend as she likes.' It did genuinely seem to him a vast sum. A guinea to fritter away!

However, towards three o'clock its vastness had shrunk.

'Dashed if I don't give the wench a fiver!' he exclaimed. It was madness, but he had an obscure feeling that he might have had more amusement if he had begun being mad rather earlier in life.

Upon this he slept soundly till six o'clock.

His mind then unfortunately got entangled in the painful episode of the ten-pound note. He and Helen had the same blood in their veins. They were alike in some essential traits. He knew that neither of them could ever persuade himself, or herself, to mention that miserable ten-pound note again. 'If I gave her a tenner,' he said, 'that would make her see as I'd settled to forget that business, and let bygones *be* bygones. I'll give her a tenner.'

It was preposterous. She could not, of course, spend it. She would put it away. So it would not be wasted.

Upon this he rose.

Poor simpleton! Ever since the commencement of his relations with Helen, surprise had followed surprise for him. And the series was not ended.

The idea of giving a gift made him quite nervous. He fumbled in his cashbox for quite a long time and then he called, nervously:

'Helen!'

She came, out of the kitchen into the front room. (Dress: White muslin – unspeakable extravagance in a town of smuts.)

'It's thy birthday, lass?'

She nodded, smiling.

'Well, tak' this.'

He handed her a ten-pound note.

'Oh, thank you, uncle!' she cried, just on the calm side of effusiveness.

At this point the surprise occurred.

There was another ten-pound note in the cashbox. His fingers went for a stroll on their own account and returned with that note.

'Hold on!' he admonished her for jumping to conclusions. 'And this!' And he gave her a second note. He was much more startled than she was.

'Oh, *thank* you uncle!' And then, laughing: 'Why, it's nearly a sovereign for every year of my life!'

'How old art?'

'Twenty-six.'

'I'm gone dotty!' he said to his soul. 'I'm gone dotty!' And his eyes watched his fingers take six sovereigns out of the box, and count them into her small white hand. And his cheek felt her kiss.

She went off with twenty-six pounds – twenty-six pounds! The episode was entirely incredible.

Breakfast was a most pleasing meal. Though acknowledging himself an imbecile, he was obliged to acknowledge also

that a certain pleasure springs from a certain sort of imbecility.
Helen was adorable.

Now that same morning he had received from Mrs. Prockter a flattering note, asking him, if he could spare the time, to
go up to Hillport and examine Wilbraham Hall with her, and
give her his expert advice as to its value, etc. He informed
Helen of the plan.

'I'll go with you,' she said at once. 'What's in the wind?' he
asked himself. He saw in the suggestion a device for seeing
Emanuel.

'The fact is,' she added, 'I want to show you a house up at
Hillport that might do for us.'

He winced. She had said nothing about a removal for quite
some time. He hated the notion of removal. ('Flitting,' he
called it.) It would mean extra expense, too. As for Hillport,
he was sure that nothing, except cottages, could be got in
Hillport for less than fifty pounds a year. If she thought he was
going to increase his rent by thirty-two pounds a year, besides
rates, she was in error. The breakfast finished in a slight mist.
He hardened. The idea of her indicating houses to him! The
idea of her assuming that — Well, no use in meeting trouble
half-way!

CHAPTER XVI

THE HALL AND ITS RESULT

'Yes,' said Mrs. Prockter, gazing about her, to James Ollerenshaw, 'it certainly is rather spacious.'

'Rather spacious!' James repeated in the secret hollows of his mind. It was not spacious; it was simply fantastic. They stood, those two – Mrs. Prockter in her usual flowered silk, and James in his usual hard rent-collecting clothes – at the foot of the double staircase, which sprang with the light of elegance of wings from the floor of the entrance-hall of Wilbraham Hall. In front of them, over the great door, was a musicians' gallery, and over that a huge window. On either side of the great door were narrow windows which looked over stretches of green country far away from the Five Towns. For Wilbraham Hall was on the supreme ridge of Hillport, and presented only its back yard, so to speak, to the Five Towns. And though the carpets were rolled up and tied with strings, and though there were dark rectangular spaces on the walls showing where pictures had been, the effect of the hall was quite a furnished effect. Polished oak and tasselled hangings, and monstrous vases and couches and chairs preserved in it the appearance of a home, if a home of giants.

Decidedly it was worthy of the mighty reputations of the extinct Wilbrahams. The Wilbrahams had gradually risen in North Staffordshire for two centuries. About the Sunday of the Battle of Waterloo they were at their apogee. Then for a century they had gradually fallen. And at last they had extinguished themselves in the person of a young-old fool who was in prison for having cheated a pawnbroker. This young-old fool had nothing but the name of Wilbraham to his back. The wealth of the Wilbrahams, or what remained of it after eight decades of declension, had, during the course of a famous twenty years' law-suit between the father of the said

84

young-old fool and a farming cousin in California, slowly settled like golden dust in the offices of lawyers in Carey-street, London. And the house, grounds, lake, and furniture (save certain portraits) were now on sale by order of the distant winner of the law-suit. And both Mrs. Prockter and James could remember the time when the twin-horsed equip-age of the Wilbrahams used to dash about the Five Towns like the chariot of the sun. The recollection made Mrs. Prockter sad, but in James it produced no such feeling. To Mrs. Prockter, Wilbraham Hall was the last of the stylish port-wine estates that in old days dotted the heights around the Five Towns. To her it was the symbol of the death of tone and the triumph of industrialism. Whereas James merely saw it as so much building land upon which streets of profitable and inexpensive semi-detached villas would one day rise at the wand's touch of the man who had sufficient audacity for a prodigious speculation.

'It 'ud be like living in th' covered market, living here,' James observed.

The St. Luke's Market is the largest roof in Bursley. And old inhabitants, incapable of recovering from the surprise of marketing under cover instead of in an open square, still, after thirty years, refer to it as the covered market.

Mrs. Prockter smiled.

'By the way,' said James, 'where's them childer?'

The old people looked around. Emanuel and Helen, who had entered the proud precincts with them, had vanished.

'I believe they're upstairs, ma'am,' said the fat caretaker, pleating her respectable white apron.

'You can go,' said Mrs. Prockter, curtly, to this vestige of grandeur. 'I will see you before I leave.'

The apron resented the dismissal, and perhaps would have taken it from none but Mrs. Prockter. But Mrs. Prockter had a mien, and a flowered silk, before which even an apron of the Wilbrahams must quail. 'I may tell you, Mr. Ollerenshaw,' she remarked, confidentially, when they were alone, 'that I have not the slightest intention of buying this place. Emanuel takes advantage of my good nature. You've no idea how persistent he is. So all you have to do is to advise me firmly not to buy it. That's why I've asked you to come up. He acknowledges that you're an authority, and he'll be forced to accept your judgment.'

'Why didn't ye say that afore, missis?' asked James, bluntly.

'Before when?'

'Before that kick-up (party) o' yours. He got out of me then as I thought it were dirt cheap at eight thousand.'

'But I don't want to move,' pleaded Mrs. Prockter.

'I'm asking ye why ye didn't tell me afore?' James repeated.

Mrs. Prockter looked at him. 'Men are trying creatures!' she said. 'So it seems you can't tell a tarradiddle for me?' And she sighed.

'I don't know as I object to that. What I object to is contradicting mysen.'

'Why did you bring Helen?' Mrs. Prockter demanded.

'I didna'. She come hersen.'

They exchanged glances.

'And now she and Emanuel have run off.'

'It looks to me,' said James 'as if your plan for knocking their two heads together wasna' turning out as you meant it, missis.'

'And what's more,' said she, 'I do believe that Emanuel wants me to buy this place so that when I'm gone he can make a big splash here with your niece and your money, Mr. Ollerenshaw! What do you think of that?'

'He may make as much splash as he's a mind to, wi' my niece,' James answered. 'But he won't make much of a splash with my money, I can promise ye.' His orbs twinkled. 'I can promise ye,' he repeated.

'To whom do you mean to leave it, then?'

'Not to *his* wife.'

'H'm! Well, as we're here, I suppose we may as well see what there is to be seen. And those two dreadful young people must be found.'

They mounted the stairs.

'Will you give me your arm, Mr. Ollerenshaw?'

To such gifts he was not used. Already he had given twenty-six pounds that day. The spectacle of Jimmy ascending the state staircase of Wilbraham Hall with all the abounding figure of Mrs. Prockter on his arm would have drawn crowds had it been offered to the public at sixpence a head.

They inspected the great drawing-room, the great dining-room, the great bedroom, and all the lesser rooms; the galleries, the balconies, the panellings, the embrasures, the suites and suites and suites of Georgian and Victorian decaying furniture; the ceilings and the cornices; the pictures and engravings (of which some hundreds remained); the ornaments, the clocks, the screens, and the microscopic knick-knacks. Both of them lost count of everything, except that before they reached the attics they had passed through forty-five separate apartments, not including linen closets. It was in one of the attics, as empty as Emanuel's head, that they discovered Emanuel and Helen, gazing at a magnificent prospect over the moorlands, with the gardens, the paddock, and Wilbraham Water immediately beneath.

'We've been looking for you everywhere,' Helen burst out. 'Oh, Mrs. Prockter; do come with me to the end of the corridor and look at three old distaffs that I've found in a cupboard!'

During the absence of the women, James Ollerenshaw contradicted himself to Emanuel for the sweet sake of Emanuel's stepmother. Little by little they descended to the earth, with continual detours and halts by Helen, who was several times lost and found.

'I've told him,' said James, quietly and proudly. 'I've told him it's no use to you unless you want to turn it into a building estate.'

They separated into two couples at the gate, with elaborate formalities on the part of Emanuel, which Uncle James more or less tried to imitate.

'Well?' murmured James, sighing relief, as they waited for the electric tram in that umbrageous and aristocratic portion of the Oldcastle Road which lies nearest to the portals of Wilbraham Hall. He was very pleased with himself, because, at the cost of his own respect, he had pleased Mrs. Prockter.

'Well?' murmured Helen, in response, tapping on the edge of the pavement the very same sunshade in whose company James had first made her acquaintance. She seemed nervous, hesitating, apprehensive.

'What about that house as ye've so kindly chosen for me?' he asked, genially. He wanted to humour her.

She looked him straight in the eyes. 'You've seen it,' said she.

'What!' he snorted. 'When han I seen it?'

'Just now,' she replied. 'It's Wilbraham Hall. I knew that Mrs. Prockter wouldn't have it. And, besides, I've made Emanuel give up all idea of it.'

He laughed, but with a strange and awful sensation in his stomach.

'A poor joke, lass!' he observed, with the laugh dead in his throat.

'It isn't a poor joke,' said she. 'It isn't a joke at all.'

'Didst thou seriously think as I should buy that there barracks to please thee?'

'Certainly,' she said, courageously 'Just that – to please me.'

'I'm right enough where I am,' he asserted grimly. 'What for should I buy Wilbraham Hall? What should I do in it?'

'Live in it.'

'Trafalgar Road's good enough for me.'

'But it isn't good enough for me,' said she.

'I wouldna' ha' minded,' he said savagely – 'I wouldna' ha' minded going into a house a bit bigger, but —'

'Nothing is big enough for me except Wilbraham Hall,' she said.

He said nothing. He was furious. It was her birthday, and he had given her six-and-twenty pounds – ten shillings a week for a year – and she had barely kissed him. And now, instantly after that amazing and mad generosity, she had the face to look cross because he would not buy Wilbraham Hall! It was inconceivable; it was unutterable. So he said nothing.

'Why shouldn't you, after all?' she resumed. 'You've got an income of nearly five thousand a year.' (Now he hated her for the mean manner in which she had wormed out of him secrets that previously he had shared with no one.) 'You don't spend the twentieth part of it. What are you going to do with it? *What are you going to do with it?* 'You're getting an old man.' (Cold horrors!) 'You can't take it with you when you leave the Five Towns, you know. Whom shall you leave your money to? You'll probably die worth a hundred thousands pounds, at this rate. You'll leave it to me, of course. Because there's nobody else for you to leave it to. Why can't you use it now, instead of wasting it in old stockings.'

'I bank my money, wench,' he hissingly put in.

'Old stockings!' she repeated, loudly. 'We could live splendidly at Wilbraham Hall on two thousand a year, and you
would still be saving nearly three thousand a year.'

He said nothing.

'Do you suppose I gave up my position at school in order to
live in a poky little hole at eighteen pounds a year? What do you
think I can do with myself all day in Trafalgar-road? Why,
nothing. There's no room even for a piano, and so my fingers
are stiffening every day. It's not life at all. Naturally it's a great
privilege,' she pursued, with a vicious inflection that reminded
him perfectly of Susan, 'for a girl like me to live with an old man
like you, all alone, with one servant and no sitting-room. But
some privileges cost too dear. The fact is, you never think of me
at all.' (And he had but just given her six-and-twenty pounds.)
'You think you've got a cheap housekeeper in me – but you
haven't. I'm a very good housekeeper – especially in a very
large house – but I'm not cheap.'

She spoke as if she had all her life been accustomed to living
in vast mansions. But James knew that, despite her fine
friends, she had never lived in anything appreciably larger
than his own dwelling. He knew there was not a house in
Sneyd Road, Longshaw, worth more than twenty-five
pounds a year. The whole outbreak was shocking and disgraceful. He scarcely recognised her.

He said nothing. And then suddenly he said: 'I shall buy no
Wilbraham Hall, lass.' His voice was final.

'You could sell it again at a profit,' said she. 'You could turn it
into a building estate' (parrot-cry caught from himself or from
Emanuel), 'and later on we could go and live somewhere else.'

'Yes,' said he; 'Buckingham Palace, likely!'

'I don't —' she began.

'I shall buy no Wilbraham Hall,' he reiterated. Greek had
met Greek.

The tram surged along and swallowed up the two Greeks.
They were alone in the tram, and they sat down opposite each
other. The conductor came and took James's money, and the
conductor had hardly turned his back when Helen snapped
with nostrils twitching:

'You're a miser, that's what you are! A regular old miser!

everyone knows that. Everyone calls you a miser. If you aren't a miser, I should like you to tell me why you live on about three pounds a week when your income is ninety pounds a week. I thought I might do you some good. I thought I might get you out of it. But it seems I can't.'

'Ah!' he snorted. It was a painful sight. Other persons boarded the car.

At tea she behaved precisely like an angel. Not the least hint in her demeanour of the ineffable affray of the afternoon. She was so sweet that he might have given her twenty-six Wilbraham Halls instead of twenty-six pounds. He spoke not. He was, in a very deep sense, upset.

She spent the evening in her room.

'Good-bye' she said the next morning, most amiably. It was after breakfast. She was hatted, gloved and sunshaded.

'What?' he exclaimed.

'Au revoir,' she said. 'All my things are packed up. I shall send for them. I think I can go back to the school. If I can't, I shall go to mother in Canada. Thank you very much for all your kindness. If I go to Canada, of course I shall come and see you before I leave.'

He let her shake his hand.

For two days he was haunted by memories of kidney omelettes and by the word 'miser.' Miser, eh? Him a miser! Him! Ephraim Tellwright was a miser — but *him!*

Then the natty servant gave notice, and Mrs. Butt called and suggested that she should resume her sway over him. But she did not employ exactly that phrase.

He longed for one of Helen's meals as a drunkard longs for alcohol.

Then Helen called, with the casual information that she was off to Canada. She was particularly sweet. She had the tact to make the interview short. The one blot on her conduct of the interview was that she congratulated him on the possible return of Mrs. Butt, of which she had heard from the natty servant.

'Good-bye, uncle,' she said.

'Good-bye.'

She had got as far as the door, when he whispered, brokenly: 'Lass —'

Helen turned quickly towards him.

CHAPTER XVII

DESCENDANTS OF MACHIAVELLI

Yes, she turned towards him with a rapid, impulsive movement, which expressed partly her sympathy for her old uncle,
and partly a feeling of joy caused by the sudden hope that he
had decided to give way and buy Wilbraham Hall after all.

And the fact was that, in his secret soul, he had decided to
give way; he had decided that Helen, together with Helen's
cooking, was worth to him the price of Wilbraham Hall. But
when he saw her brusque, eager gesture, he began to reflect.
His was a wily and profound nature; he reckoned that he could
read the human soul, and he said to himself:

'The wench isn't so set on leaving me as I thought she was.'

And instead of saying to her: 'Helen, lass, if you'll stop you
shall have your Wilbraham Hall,' in tones of affecting, sad
surrender, he said:

'I'm sorry to lose thee, my girl; but what must be must.'

And when he caught the look in her eyes, he was more than
ever convinced that he would be able to keep Helen without
satisfying her extremely expensive whim.

Helen, for her part, began to suspect that if she played the
fish with sufficient skill, she would capture it. Thus they both,
in a manner of speaking, got out their landing-nets.

'I don't say,' James Ollerenshaw proceeded, in accents
calculated to prove to her that he had just as great a horror of
sentimentality as she had – 'I don't say as you wouldn't make a
rare good mistress o' Wilbraham Hall. I don't say as I
wouldn't like to see you in it. But when a man reaches my age,
he's fixed in his habits like. And, what's more, supposing I *am*
saving a bit o' money, who am I saving it for, if it isn't for you
and your mother? You said as much yourself. I might pop off
any minute —'

'Uncle!' Helen protested.

'Ay, any minute!' he repeated firmly. 'I've known stronger men nor me pop off as quick as a bottle o' ginger-beer near the fire.' Here he gazed at her, and his gaze said: 'If I popped off here and now, wouldn't you feel ashamed o' yerself for being so hard on your old uncle?'

'You'll live many and many a year yet,' Helen smiled.

He shook his head pessimistically. 'I've set my heart,' he continued, 'on leaving a certain sum for you and yer mother. I've had it in mind since I don't know when. It's a fancy o' mine. And I canna' do it if I'm to go all around th' Five Towns buying barracks.'

Helen laughed. 'What a man you are for exaggerating!' she flattered him. Then she sat down.

He considered that he was gradually winding in his line with immense skill. 'Ay,' he ejaculated, with an absent air, 'it's a fancy o' mine.'

'How much do you want to leave?' Helen questioned, faintly smiling.

'Don't you bother your head about that,' said he. 'You may take it from me as it's a tidy sum. And when I'm dead and gone, and you've got it all, then ye can do as ye feel inclined.'

'I shall beat her, as sure as eggs!' he told himself.

'All this means that he'll give in when it comes to the point,' she told herself.

And aloud she said: 'Have you had supper, uncle?'

'No,' he replied.

The next development was that, without another word, she removed her gloves, lifted her pale hands to her head and slowly drew hatpins from her hat. Then she removed her hat, and plunged the pins into it again. He could scarcely refrain from snatching off his own tasselled Turkish cap and pitching it in the air. He felt as if he had won the Battle of Hastings, or defeated the captain of the bowling club in a single-handed match.

'And to think,' he reflected, 'that I should ha' given in to her by this time if I hadn't got more sense in my little finger than —' etc.

'I think I'll stay and cook you a bit of supper,' said Helen. 'I suppose Georgiana is in the kitchen?'

'If her isn't, her's in the back entry,' said Jimmy.

'What's she doing in the back entry?'

'Counting the stars,' said Jimmy; 'and that young man as comes with the bread helping her, most like.'

'I must talk to that girl.' Helen rose.

'Ye may,' said Jimmy. 'but th' baker's man'll have th' last word, or times is changed.'

He was gay. He could not conceal his gaiety. He saw himself freed from the menace of the thraldom of Mrs. Butt. He saw himself gourmandising over the meals that Helen alone could cook. He saw himself trotting up and down the streets of Bursley with the finest, smartest lass in the Five Towns by his side. And scarcely a penny of extra expenditure! And all this happy issue due to his diplomatic and histrionic skill! The fact was, Helen really liked him. There could be no doubt about that. She liked him, and she would not leave him. Also, she was a young woman of exceptional commonsense, and, being such, she would not risk the loss of a large fortune merely for the sake of indulging pique engendered by his refusal to gratify a ridiculous caprice.

Before she had well quitted the room he saw with clearness that he was quite the astutest man in the world, and that Helen was clay in his hands.

The sound of crockery in the scullery, and the cheerful little explosion when the gas-ring was ignited, and the lower mutter of conversation that ensued between Helen and Georgiana – these phenomena were music to the artist in him. He extracted the concertina from its case and began to play 'The Dead March in Saul.' Not because his sentiments had a foundation in the slightest degree funereal, but because he could perform 'The Dead March in Saul' with more virtuosity than any other piece except 'The Hallelujah Chorus.' And he did not desire to insist too much on his victory by filling Trafalgar Road with 'The Hallelujah Chorus.' He was discretion itself.

When she came back to the parlour (astoundingly natty in a muslin apron of Georgiana's) to announce supper, she made no reference to the concert which she was interrupting. He abandoned the concertina gently, caressing it into its leather shell. He was full to the brim with kindliness. It seemed to him that his life with Helen was commencing all over again.

Then he followed the indications of his nose, which already for some minutes had been prophesying to him that in the concoction of the supper Helen had surpassed herself.

And she had. There was kidney. . . . No, not in an omelette, but impaled on a skewer. A novel species of kidney, a particularity in kidneys!

'Where didst pick this up, lass?' he asked.

'It's the kidneys of that rabbit that you've bought for tomorrow,' said she.

Now, he had no affection for rabbit as an article of diet, and he had only bought the rabbit because the rabbit happened to be going past his door (in the hands of a hawker) that morning. His perfunctory purchase of it showed how he had lost interest in life and meals since Helen's departure. And lo! she had transformed a minor part of it into something wondrous, luscious, and unforgettable. Ah, she was Helen! And she was his!

'I've asked Georgiana to make up my bed,' Helen said, after the divine repast.

'I'll tell ye what I'll do' he said, in an ecstasy of generosity, 'I'll buy thee a piano, lass, and we'll put it in th' parlour against the wall where them books are now.'

She kept silence – a silence which vaguely disturbed him.

So that he added: 'And if ye're bent on a bigger house, there's one up at Park Road, above th' Park, semi-detached – at least, it's the end of a terrace – as I can get for thirty pounds a year.'

'My dearest uncle,' she said, in a firm, even voice, 'What *are* you talking about? Didn't I tell you when I came in that I had settled to go to Canada? I thought it was all decided. Surely you don't think I'm going to live in a poky house in Park Road – the very street where my school was, too! I perfectly understand that you won't buy Wilbraham Hall. That's all right. I shan't pout. I hate women who pout. We can't agree, but we're friends. You do what you like with your money, and I do what I like with myself. I had a sort of idea I would try to make you beautifully comfortable just for the last time before I left England, and that's why I'm staying. I do hope you didn't imagine anything else, uncle. There!'

She kissed him, not as a niece, but as a wise, experienced

nurse might have kissed a little boy. For she, too, in her way, reckoned herself somewhat of a diplomatist and a descendant of Machiavelli. She had thought: 'It's a funny thing if I can't bring him to his knees with a tasty supper – just to make it clear to him what he'll lose if he loses me.'

James Ollerenshaw had no sleep that night. And Helen had but little.

CHAPTER XVIII

CHICANE

He came downstairs early, as he had done after a previous sleepless night – also caused by Helen.

That it would be foolish, fatuous, and inexcusable to persevere further in his obstinacy against Helen, this he knew. He saw clearly that all his arguments to her about money and the saving of money were ridiculous; they would not have carried conviction even to the most passive intelligence, and Helen's intelligence was far from passive. They were not even true in fact, for he had never intended to leave any money to Helen's mother; he had never intended to leave any money to anybody, simply because he had not cared to think of his own decease; he had made no plans about the valuable fortune which, as Helen had too forcibly told him, he would not be able to bear away with him when he left Bursley for ever; this subject was not pleasant to him. All his rambling sentences to Helen (which he had thought so clever when he uttered them) were merely an excuse for not parting with money – money that was useless to him.

On the other hand, what Helen had said was both true and convincing; at any rate, it convinced him.

He was a miser; he admitted it. Being a miser, he saw, was one way of enjoying yourself, but not the best way. Again, if he really desired to enrich Helen, how much better to enrich her at once than at an uncertain date when he would be dead. Dead people can't be thanked. Dead people can't be kissed. Dead people can't have curious dainties offered to them for their supper. He wished to keep Helen; but Helen would only stay on one condition. That condition was a perfectly easy condition for him to fulfil. After paying eight thousand pounds (or a bit less) for Wilbraham Hall, he would still have about ten times as much money as he could possibly require.

Of course, eight thousand pounds was a lot of coin. But, then, you can't measure women (especially when they are good cooks), in terms of coin. For instance, it happened that he had exactly £8,000 in shares of the London and North Western Railway Company. The share-certificates were in his safe; he could hold them in his hand; he could sell them and buy Wilbraham Hall with the proceeds. That is to say, he could exchange them for Helen. Now, it would be preposterous to argue that he would not derive more satisfaction from Helen than from those crackling share-certificates.

Wilbraham Hall, once he became its owner, would be a worry – an awful worry. Well, would it? Would not Helen be entirely capable of looking after it, of superintending it in every way? He knew that she would! As for the upkeep of existence in Wilbraham Hall, had not Helen proved to him that its cost was insignificant when compared to his income? She had.

And as to his own daily manner of living, could he not live precisely as he chose at Wilbraham Hall? He could. It was vast; but nothing would compel him to live in all of it at once. He could choose a nice little room, and put a notice on the door that it was not to be disturbed. And Helen could run the rest of the mansion as her caprice dictated.

The process of argument was over when Helen descended to put the finishing touches to a breakfast which she had evidently concocted with Georgiana the night before.

'Breakfast is ready, uncle' she called to him.

He obeyed. Flowers on the table once more! The first since her departure! A clean cloth! A general, inexplicable tuning-up of the meal's frame.

You would now, perhaps, have expected him to yield, as gracefully as an old man can. He wanted to yield. He hungered to yield. He knew that it was utterly for his own good to yield. But if you seriously expected him to yield, your knowledge of human nature lacks depth. Something far stronger than argument, something far stronger than desire for his own happiness, prevented him from yielding. Pride, a silly self-conceit, the greatest enemy of the human race, forbade him to yield. For, on the previous night, Helen had snubbed him – and not for the first time. He could not accept the snub with meekness, though it would have paid him handsomely to do so, though as a Christian and a philosopher he ought to have done so. He could not.

So he put on a brave face, pretended to accept the situation with contented calm, and talked as if Canada was the next street, and as if her going was entirely indifferent to him. Helen imitated him.

It was a lovely morning; not a cloud in the sky – only in their hearts.

'Uncle!' she said after breakfast was done and cleared away.

He was counting rents in his cashbox in the front parlour, and she had come to him, and was leaning over his shoulder.

'Well, lass?'

'Have you got twenty-five pounds in that box?'

It was obvious that he had.

'I shouldna' be surprised,' said he.

'I wish you'd lend it me.'

'What for?'

'I want to go over to Hanbridge and book my berth, definitely, and I've no loose cash.'

Now here was a chance to yield. But no.

'Dost mean to say,' he exclaimed, 'as ye havena' booked yer berth? When does th' steamer sail?'

'There's one from Glasgow next Saturday,' said she – 'the *Saskatchewan*. I secured the berth, but I didn't pay for it.'

'It's a rare lot of money,' he observed.

'Oh,' she said, 'I didn't want all that for the fare. I've other things to pay for – railway to Glasgow, etc. You will lend it me, won't you?' her fingers were already in the cashbox. She was behaving just like a little girl, like a spoilt child. It was remarkable, he considered, how old and mature Helen could be when she chose, and how kittenish when she chose.

She went off with four five-pound notes and five sovereigns. 'Will you ask me to come back and cook the dinner?' she smiled, ironically, enchantingly.

'Ay!' he said. He was bound to smile also.

She returned in something over two hours.

'There you are!' she said, putting a blue-green paper into his hand. 'Ever seen one of these before?'

It was the ticket for the steamer.

This staggered him. A sensible, determined woman, who disappears to buy a steamer-ticket, may be expected to reappear with a steamer-ticket. And yet it staggered him. He could scarcely believe it. She was going, then! She was going! It was inevitable now.

'The boat leaves the Clyde at ten in the morning,' she said, resuming possession of the paper, 'so we must go to Glasgow on Friday, and stop the night at an hotel.'

'We?' he murmured, aghast.

'Well,' she said, 'you surely won't let me travel to Glasgow all alone, will you?'

'Her's a caution, her is!' he privately reflected.

'You can come back on Saturday,' she said; 'so that you'll be in time to collect your rents. There's an express to Glasgow from Crewe at 1.15, and to catch that we must take the 12.20 at Shawport.'

She had settled every detail.

'And what about my dinner?' he inquired. 'I'm going to set about it instantly,' laughed she.

'I mean my dinner on Friday?' he said.

'Oh, *that!*' she replied. 'There's a restaurant-car from Crewe. So we can lunch on the train.'

This idea of accompanying her to Glasgow pleased him intensely. 'Glasgow isna' much i' my line,' he said. 'But you wenches do as ye like, seemingly.'

Thus, on the Friday morning, he met her down at Shawport Station. He was in his best clothes, but he had walked. She arrived in a cab, that carried a pagoda of trunks on its fragile roof; she had come straight from her lodgings. There was a quarter of an hour before train-time. He paid for the cab. He also bought one second-class single and one second-class return to Glasgow, while she followed the porter who trundled her luggage. When he came out of the booking-office (minus several gold pieces), she was purchasing papers at the bookstall, and farther up the platform the porter had seized a paste-brush, and was opening a cupboard of labels. An extraordinary scheme presented itself to James Ollerenshaw's mind, and he trotted up to the porter.

'I've seen to the baggage myself,' said Helen, without looking at him.

'All right,' he said.

The porter touched his cap.

'Label that luggage for Crewe,' he whispered to the porter, and passed straight on as if taking exercise on the platform.

'Yes, sir,' said the porter.

When he got back to Helen of course he had to make conversation with a nonchalant air, in order to hide his guilty feelings.

'So none of 'em has come to see you off!' he observed.

'None of whom?'

'None o' yer friends.'

'No fear!' she said. 'I wouldn't have it for anything. I do hate and loathe good-byes at a railway station. Don't you?'

'Never had any,' he said.

The train was prompt, but between Shawport and Crewe it suffered delays, so that there was not an inordinate amount of time to spare at the majestic junction.

Heedless, fly-away creature that she was, Helen scurried from the North Stafford platform to the main-line platform without a thought as to her luggage. She was apparently so preoccupied with her handbag, which contained her purse, that she had no anxiety left over for her heavy belongings.

As they hastened forward, he saw the luggage being tumbled out on to the platform.

The Glasgow train rolled grandiosely in, and the restaurant-car came to a standstill almost exactly opposite the end of the North Stafford platform. They obtained two seats with difficulty. Then, as there was five minutes to wait, Jimmy descended from the car to the asphalte and peeped down the North Stafford platform. Yes, her luggage was lying there, deserted, in a pile. He remained in the carriage.

'I suppose the luggage will be all right?' Helen said, calmly, just as the guard whistled.

'Ay!' said he, with the mien of a traveller of vast experience. 'I saw 'em bringing all th' N.S. luggage over. It were th' fust thing I thought of.'

As a liar he reckoned he was pretty good.

He glanced from the window as the train slid away from Crewe, and out of the tail of his eye, in the distance, over the heads of people, he had a momentary glimpse of the topmost of Helen's trunks safely at rest on the North Stafford platform.

He felt safe. He felt strangely joyous.

He ate largely, and made very dry, humorous remarks about the novelty of a restaurant on wheels.

'Bless us!' he said, as the express flashed through Preston without stopping. 'It's fust time as I've begun a bottle o' Bass in one town and finished it in another.'

He grew positively jolly, and the journey seemed to be accomplished with the rapidity of a dream.

CHAPTER XIX

THE TOSSING

'You said you'd seen it into the van,' pouted Helen – she who never pouted!

'Nay, lass,' he corrected her, 'I said I'd seen 'em bringing all th' luggage over.'

The inevitable moment of reckoning had arrived. They stood together on the platform of St. Enoch's, Glasgow. The last pieces of luggage were being removed from the guard's van under the direction of passengers, and there was no sign whatever of Helen's trunks. This absence of Helen's trunks did not in the least surprise James Ollerenshaw; he was perfectly aware that Helen's trunks reposed, at that self-same instant, in the lost luggage office at Crewe; but, of course, he had to act surprise. In case of necessity he could act very well. It was more difficult for him to act sorrow than to act surprise; but he did both to his own satisfaction. He climbed into the van and scanned its corners – in vain. Then, side by side, they visited the other van at the head of the train, with an equal result.

The two guards, being Scotch, responded to inquiries with extreme caution. All that they would answer for was that the trunks were not in the train. Then the train was drawn out of the station by a toy-engine, and the express engine followed it with grave dignity, and Helen and Jimmy were left staring at the empty rails.

'Something must be done,' said Helen, crossly.

'Ay!' Jimmy agreed. 'It's long past my tea-time. We must find out if there's anything to eat i' Scotland.'

But Helen insisted on visiting the station-master. Now, the stationmaster at St. Enoch's is one of the most important personages north of the Tweed, and not easily to be seen. However, Helen saw him. He pointed out that the train came from London in two portions, which were divided in Scot-

102

land, one going to Edinburgh, and his suggestion was that conceivably the luggage had been put into the Edinburgh van in mistake for the Glasgow van. Such errors did occur sometimes, he said, implying that the North Western was an English railway, and that surprising things happened in England. He said, also, that Helen might telephone to Edinburgh to inquire.

She endeavoured to act on this counsel, but came out of the telephone cabin saying that she could not get into communication with Edinburgh.

'Better go over to Edinburgh and see for yourself,' said Jimmy, tranquilly.

'Yes, and what about my steamer?' Helen turned on him.

'Scotland canna' be so big as all that,' said Jimmy. 'Not according to th' maps. Us could run over to Edinburgh to-night, and get back to Glasgow early to-morrow.'

She consented.

Just as he was taking two second returns to Edinburgh (they had snatched railway eggs and railway tea while waiting for a fast train) he stopped and said:

'Unless ye prefer to sail without your trunks, and I could send 'em on by th' next steamer?'

'Uncle,' she protested, 'I do wish you wouldn't be so silly. The idea of me sailing without my trunks! Why don't you ask me to sail without my head?'

'All right – all right!' he responded. 'But don't snap mine off. Two second returns to Edinburgh, young man, and I'll thank ye to look slippy over it.'

In the Edinburgh train he could scarcely refrain from laughing. And Helen, too, seemed more in a humour to accept the disappearance of five invaluable trunks, full of preciosities, as a facetious sally on the part of destiny.

He drew out a note-book which he always carried, and did mathematical calculations.

'That makes twenty-seven pounds eighteen and ninepence as ye owe me,' he remarked.

'What? For railway tickets?'

'Railway tickets, tips, and that twenty-five pounds I lent ye. I'm making ye a present of *my* fares, and dinner, and tea and so forth'

'Twenty-five pounds that you lent me!' she murmured.

'Yes,' he said. 'Tuesday morning, while I was at my cashbox.'

'Oh, *that*!' she ejaculated. 'I thought you were giving me that. I never thought you'd ask me for it again, uncle. I'd completely forgotten all about it.'

She seemed quite sincere in this amazing assertion.

His acquaintance with the ways of women was thus enlarged, suddenly, and at the merely nominal expense of twenty-five pounds. It was a wondrous proof of his high spirits and his general contentedness with himself that he should have submitted to the robbery without a groan.

'What's twenty-five pun'?' he reflected. 'There'll be no luggage for her at Edinburgh; that steamer'll go without her; and then I shall give in. I shall talk to her about the ways o' Providence, and tell her it's borne in upon me as she must have Wilbraham Hall if she's in a mind to stay. I shall save my face, anyhow.'

And he further decided that, in case of necessity, in case of Helen at a later stage pushing her inquiries as to the luggage inconveniently far he would have to bribe the porter at Shawport to admit to her that he, the porter, had made a mistake in the labelling.

When they had satisfied themselves that Edinburgh did not contain Helen's trunks – no mean labour, for the lost luggage office was closed, and they had to move mountains in order to get it opened on the plea of extremest urgency – Jimmy Ollerenshaw turned to Susan's daughter, saying to himself that she must be soothed regardless of cost. Miracles would not enable her to catch the steamer now, and the hour was fast approaching when he would benevolently offer her the gift of Wilbraham Hall.

'Well, lass,' he began, 'I'm right sorry. What's to be done?'

'There's nothing at all to be done,' she replied, smiling sadly. She might have upbraided him for carelessness in the matter of the luggage. She might have burst into tears and declared passionately that it was all *his* fault. But she did not. 'Except, of course, that I must cable to mother. She's coming to Quebec to meet me.'

'That'll do to-morrow,' he said. 'What's to be done to-night? In th' way o' supper, as ye might say?'

'We must go to an hotel. I believe the station hotel is the best.' She pointed to a sign and a directing black hand which said: 'To the hotel.'

In a minute James Ollerenshaw found himself in the largest and most gorgeous hotel in Scotland.

'Look here, wench,' he said. 'I don't know as this is much in my line. Summat a thought less gaudy 'll do for my old bones.'

'I won't move a step farther this night!' Helen declared. 'I'm ready to drop.'

He remembered that she must be soothed.

'Well,' he said, 'here goes!'

And he strode across the tessellated pavement under the cold, scrutinizing eye of menials to a large window marked in gold letters: 'Bureau.'

'Have ye gotten a couple of bedrooms like?' he asked the clerk.

'Yes, sir,' said the clerk (who was a perfect lady). 'What do you want?'

'Don't I tell ye as we want a couple o' bedrooms, miss?'

After negotiations she pushed across the counter to him, – two discs of cardboard numbered 324 and 326, each marked 6s. 6d. He regarded the price as fantastic, but no cheaper rooms were to be had, and Helen's glance was dangerous.

'Why,' he muttered, 'I've got a four-roomed cottage empty at Turnill as I'd let for a month for thirteen shillings, *and* paper it!'

'Where is your luggage sir?' asked a muscular demon with shiny sleeves.

'That's just what we want to know, young feller,' said Jimmy. 'For the present, that's all as we can lay our hands on.' And he indicated Helen's satchel.

His experiences in the lift were exciting, and he suggested the laying of a tramway along the corridor of the fourth floor. The beautiful starched creature who brought in his hot water (without being asked) found him in the dark struggling with the electric light, which he had extinguished from curiosity and had not been able to rekindle, having lost the location of the switch.

At 10.30 the travellers were seated at a table in the immense dining-room, which was populated by fifteen waiters of various European nationalities, and six belated guests including themselves. The one item on the menu which did not exceed his comprehension was Welsh rarebit, and he ordered it.

It was while they were waiting in anticipation of this dish that he decided to commence operations upon Helen. The fact was, he was becoming very anxious to put affairs on a definite footing.

'Well, my girl,' he said, 'cheer up. If ye tak' my advice ye'll make up yer mind to stop i' owd England with yer owd uncle.'

'Of course I will,' she answered, softly: and added: 'If you'll do as I want.'

'Buy that barracks?'

She nodded.

He was on the very point of yielding; he was on the very point of saying, with a grand-fatherly, god-like tone of utter beneficence: 'Lass, ye shall have it. I wouldn't ha' given it ye, but it's like as if what must be – this luggage being lost. It's like as if Providence was in it.' He was on the very point of this decisive pronouncement, when a novel and dazzling idea flashed into his head.

'Listen here,' he said, bending across the table towards her, 'I'll toss thee.'

'Toss me?' she exclaimed, startled.

'Ay! I'll toss thee, if thou'lt stay. Heads I buy the barracks; tails I don't, and you live with me in a *house*.'

'Very well,' she agreed, lightly.

He had not really expected her to agree to such a scheme. But then young women named Helen can be trusted absolutely to falsify expectation. He took a sixpence from his pocket.

'Heads I win, eh?' he said.

She acquiesced, and up went the sixpence.

It rolled off the table on to the Turkey carpet (Jimmy was not so adroit as he had been in his tossing days), and seven Austrians, Germans, and Swiss sprang towards it with a simultaneous impulse to restore it to its owner.

Jimmy jumped to his feet.

'Don't touch it!' he cried, and bent over it.

'Nay, nay!' he muttered, 'I've lost. Th' old man's lost, after all!'

And he returned to the table, having made a sensation in the room.

Helen was in paradise. 'I'm surprised you were ready to toss, uncle,' said she. 'However, it's all right; we can get the luggage to-morrow. It's at Crewe.'

'How dost know it's at Crewe?' he demanded.

'Because I had it labelled for Crewe. You *were* silly to imagine that I was going to leave you. But I thought I'd just leave nothing undone to make you give way. I made sure I was beaten. And now you are goose enough to toss, and you've lost, you've lost! Hurrah!' She clapped her hands softly.

'Do ye mean to tell me,' Jimmy thundered, 'As ye've been playing a game wi' me all this time?' She had no shame.

'And bought th' steamer-ticket without meaning to go?'

'Well,' she said, 'it's no good half-playing when you're playing for high stakes. Besides, what's fifteen pounds?'

He did not let her into the secret that he also had ordered the luggage to be labelled for Crewe. They returned to the Five Towns the following morning. And by mutual tacit agreement they never spoke of that excursion to Scotland.

In such manner came Helen Rathbone to be the mistress of Wilbraham Hall.

CHAPTER XX

THE FLITTING

Before the spacious crimson façade of Wilbraham Hall upon an autumn day stood Mr. Crump's pantechnicon. That is to say, it was a pantechnicon only by courtesy – Mr. Crump's courtesy. In strict adherence to truth it was just a common furniture-removing van, dragged over the earth's surface by two horses. On the outer walls of it were an announcement that Mr. Crump removed goods by road, rail or steamer, and vast coloured pictures of Mr. Crump removing goods by road, rail and steamer. One saw the van in situations of grave danger – travelling on an express train over a lofty viaduct at sixty miles an hour or rolling on the deck of a steamer in a stormy sea. One saw it also in situations of impressive natural beauty – as, for instance, passing by road through terrific mountain defiles, where cataracts rushed and foamed. The historic fact was that the van had never been beyond the Five Towns. Nevertheless, Mr. Crump bound himself in painted letters six inches high to furnish estimates for any removal whatsoever; and, what is more, as a special boon to the Five Towns, to furnish estimates free of charge. In this detail Mr. Crump had determined not to lag behind his fellow-furniture-removers, who, one and all, persist in refusing to accept even a small fee for telling you how much they demand for their services.

In the van were the entire worldly possessions of James Ollerenshaw (except his houses, his investments, a set of bowls up at the bowling club, and the clothes he wore), and the entire worldly possessions of Helen Rathbone (except the clothes she wore). If it be asked where was the twenty-six pounds so generously given to her by a loving uncle, the reply is that the whole sum together with much else, was in the coffers of Ezra Brunt, the draper and costumier at Hanbridge;

and the reply further is that Helen was in debt. I have hitherto concealed Helen's tendency to debts, but it was bound sooner or later to come out. And here it is.

After an adventurous journey by bridge over the North Staffordshire Railway, and by bridge over the foaming catar-act of the Shaws Brook, and down the fearful slants of Oldcastle Street, and through the arduous terrific defiles of Oldcastle Road, the van had arrived at the portals of Wilbra-ham Hall. It would have been easy, by opening wide the portals, to have introduced the van and the horses too into the hall of Wilbraham Hall. But this course was not adopted.

Helen and Georgiana had preceded the van and they both stood at the door to receive the goods. Georgiana was in one of Georgiana's aprons, and Helen also was in one of Geor-giana's aprons. Uncle James had followed the van. He had not let it out of his sight. The old man's attachment to even the least of his goods was touching, and his attachment to the greatest of his goods carried pathos into farce. The greatest of his goods was, apparently, the full-rigged ship and tempes-tuous ocean in a glass box which had stood on the table in the front room of the other house for many years. No one had suspected his esteem for that glass box and its contents. He had not suspected it himself until the moment for packing it had come. But he seemed to love it more than his bits of Spode china or his concertina; and, taking it with him, he had quitted with a softened regret the quantity of over-blown blue roses which, in their eternal bloom, had enlivened his exist-ence during a longer period even than the ship and ocean.

The ship and ocean was the last thing put into the van and the first thing taken out, and James Ollerenshaw introduced the affair, hugged against his own breast, into the house of his descendants. The remainder of the work of transference was relatively unimportant. Two men accomplished it easily while the horses ate a late dinner. And then the horses and the van and the men went off, and there was nothing left but a few wisps of straw and so forth, on the magnificent sweep of gravel, to indicate that they had ever been there. And Uncle James, and Helen and Georgiana felt rather forlorn and abandoned. They stood in the hall and looked at each other a little blankly, like gipsies camping out in an abandoned cathedral. An immense fire was burning in the immense fireplace of the hall, and similar fires were burning in the state bedroom, in a little drawing-room beyond the main drawing-room, in another bedroom, in the giant's kitchen, and in one of the attics. These fires and a certain amount of cleaning were the only preparations which Helen had permitted herself to make. Even the expense of the coal had startled James, and she proposed to get him safely in the cage before commencing the serious business which would shatter all his nerves. By a miracle of charm, and audacity she had obtained from him the control of a sum of seven hundred and fifty pounds. This sum, now lying nominally to her credit at one of James's various banks, represented the difference between eight thousand pounds (at which James had said Wilbraham Hall would be cheap) and seven thousand two hundred and fifty pounds (at which James had succeeded in buying Wilbraham Hall).

To the left of the Hall, near the entrance, was quite a small room (originally, perhaps a butler's lair), and James was obstinate in selecting this room as his office. He had his desk carried there, and everything that personally affected him, except his safe and the simple necessaries of his bedroom. These were taken, not to the state bedroom, which he had declined, after insincere pressure from Helen to accept it, but to a much smaller sleeping-chamber. The numerous family of Windsor chairs, together with other ancient honesties, were sent up to attics – too old at forty! Georgiana was established in a glorious attic; the state bedroom was strewn with Helen's gear; and scarcely anything remained unniched in the Hall save the ship and ocean. They all rested from their labours, and Helen was moved by one of her happiest inspirations.

'Georgiana,' she said, 'go and make some tea. Bring a cup for yourself.'

'Yes, miss. Thank you, miss.'

On removal days miserable distinctions of class are invariably lost in the large-heartedness of mutual endeavour.

It was while the trio were thus drinking tea together, standing, and, as it were, with loins still girt after the pilgrimage, that the first visitor to the new owners of Wilbraham Hall rang its great bell and involved Georgiana in her first ceremonial duty. Georgiana was quite nervous as she went to the door.

The caller was Emanuel Prockter.

'Mother thought I might perhaps be able to help you,' said he, in the slightly simpering tone which he adopted in delicate situations, and which he thought suited him. What made the situation delicate, to him, was Helen's apron – quite agreeable though the apron was. He felt, with his unerring perceptiveness, that young ladies do not care to receive young gentlemen in the apron of a Georgiana. His own attire was, as usual, fabulously correct; the salient features of it being a pair of light yellow chamois gloves, loose-fitting and unbuttoned, with the gauntlets negligently turned back. These gloves were his method of expressing the fact that the visit was a visit of usefulness and not a kid-glove visit. But Helen seemed quite composed behind Georgiana's apron.

'Yes,' he repeated, with smiling inanity, after he had shaken hands. 'Mother thought I might help you.'

('What a fool that woman is!' reflected James. 'And what a fool *he* is to put it on to his mother instead of keeping it to himself!')

'And what did *you* think, Mr. Prockter?' Helen demanded. 'Another cup and saucer, Georgiana.'

Helen's question was one of her insolent questions.

('Perhaps his mother ain't such a fool!' reflected James. And he perceived, or imagined he perceived, that their fears of Helen marrying Emanuel were absurd.)

Emanuel sniffed humour in the air. He never understood humour; but he was, at any rate, sufficiently gifted with the wisdom of the simple to smile vaguely and amiably when he sniffed humour.

And then Helen said, with cordial kindliness: 'It's awfully good of you – awfully good of you. Here we are, you see!'

And the degree of cordiality was such that the fear of her marrying Emanuel suddenly seemed less absurd to James. The truth was that James never had a moment's peace of mind with Helen. She was continually proving that as a student in the University of Human Nature he had not even matriculated.

Georgiana appeared with an odd cup and saucer, and a giggling statement that she had not been able to discover any more teaspoons.

'Never mind,' said Helen. 'Mr. Prockter shall have mine.'

('Well, I'm hanged!' reflected James.)

Whereupon Georgiana departed, bearing her own tea, into the giant's kitchen. The miserable distinctions of class had been mysteriously established.

CHAPTER XXI

SHIP AND OCEAN

The host, the hostess, and the guest all remained on their feet in the noble hall of the Wilbrahams, it not being good etiquette to sit at removals, even when company calls. Emanuel, fortunately for him, was adept at perambulation with a full cup of tea in one hand and a hat or so in the other. There were two things which he really could do – one was to sing a sentimental song without laughing, and the other was to balance a cup of tea. And it was only when he was doing the one or the other that he genuinely lived. During the remainder of his existence he was merely a vegetable inside a waistcoat. He held his cup without a tremor while Helen charmingly introduced into it her tea-spoon and stirred up the sugar. Then, after he had sipped and pronounced the result excellent, he began to admire the Hall and the contents of the Hall. A proof of his real Christian charity was that, whereas he had meant to have that Hall for himself, he breathed no word of envy nor discontent. He praised everything; and presently he arrived at the ship and ocean, and praised that. He particularly praised the waves.

The heart of James instantly and instinctively softened towards him. For the realism of those foaming waves had always struck James as the final miracle of art. And, moreover, this was the first time that any of Helen's haughty 'set' had ever deigned to recognise the merits of the ship and ocean.

'Where shouldst hang it, Master Prockter?' James genially asked.

'Hang it, uncle?' exclaimed Helen. 'Are you going to hang it? Aren't you going to keep it on the table in your own room?'

She was hoping that it might occupy a position not too

prominent. She did not intend it to be the central decorative attraction of the palace.

'It ought to be hung,' said Emanuel. 'See, here are the little iron things for the nails.'

This gift of observation pleased James. Emanuel was indeed beginning to show quite an intelligent interest in the ship and ocean.

'Of course it must be hung,' said he.

He was very human, was Jimmy Ollerenshaw. For at least twenty-five years he had possessed the ship and ocean, and cherished it, always meaning one day to hang it against the wall as it deserved. And yet he had never arrived at doing so, though the firm resolution to do so had not a whit weakened in his mind. And now he was absolutely decided, with the whole force of his will behind him, to hang the ship and ocean at once.

'There! Under the musicians' gallery wouldn't be a bad place, would it, Mr. Ollerenshaw?' Emanuel suggested, respectfully.

James trained his eye on the spot. 'The very thing, lad!' said he, with enthusiasm.

'Lad!' Helen had not recovered from a private but extreme astonishment at this singular mark of paternal familiarity to Emanuel when there was another and a far louder ring at the door.

Georgiana minced and tripped out of her retreat, and opened the majestic portal to a still greater surprise for Helen. The ringer was Mr. Andrew Dean – Mr. Andrew Dean with his dark, quasi-hostile eyes, and his heavy shoulders, and his defiant, suspicious bearing – Mr. Andrew Dean in workaday clothes and with hands that could not be called clean. Andrew stared about him like a scout, and then advanced rapidly to Helen and seized her hand, hurting it.

'I was just passing,' said he, in a hoarse voice. 'I expect you'd be in a bit of a mess, so I thought I might be useful. How d'ye do, Mr. Ollerenshaw?' And he hurt James's hand also.

'It's very kind of you,' Helen remarked, flushing.

'How do, Prockter?' Andrew jerked out at Emanuel, not taking his hand.

This abstention on Andrew's part from physical violence was capable of two interpretations. The natural interpretation was that Andrew's social methods were notoriously casual and capricious. The interesting interpretation was that a failure of the negotiations between Emanuel and Andrew for a partnership – a failure which had puzzled Bursley – had left rancour behind it. •

Emanuel, however, displayed no symptom of being disturbed. His blandness remained intact. Nevertheless, the atmosphere was mysteriously electric. Helen felt it to be so, and an atmosphere which is deemed to be electric by even one person only, *ipso facto,* is electric. As for James Ollerenshaw, he was certainly astonished by the visit of Andrew Dean; but, being absorbed in the welfare of his ship and ocean, he permitted his astonishment to dissolve in a vague satisfaction that, anyhow, Helen's unexplained quarrel with Andrew Dean was really at an end. This call was assuredly Andrew's way of expiatory repentance.

'The very thing!' he repeated, glancing at Emanuel as if in expectation.

Emanuel did not seem to comprehend that aught was expected of him. He amiably stood, with hands still appropriately gloved and his kindly glance wandered between the ship and ocean and the spot which he had hit on for the ship and ocean's last resting-place.

'Where's th' steps, Helen?' James inquired, and, after a brief silence: 'Georgiana!' he yelled.

The girl flew in.

'Bring us a pair o' steps,' said he.

Followed an unsuccessful search for the pair of steps, which Andrew Dean ultimately discovered in a corner of the hall itself, lying flat behind a vast roll of carpet which was included in the goods purchased for seven thousand two hundred and fifty pounds. The steps being found, Georgiana explained at length how she distinctly remembered seeing one of the men put them behind the roll of carpet.

'Now, what is it?' Andrew vigorously questioned. He was prepared, evidently, to do anything that a man may do with a pair of steps. When the operation was indicated to him, his first act was to take off his coat, which he threw on the floor.

'Hammer! Nails!' he ejaculated. And Georgiana, intimidated by his tone, contrived to find both hammer and nails. It is true that the hammer was a coal hammer.

And in a remarkably short space of time he was balanced on the summit of the steps with a nail in one hand, a hammer in the other, a pencil behind his ear, and another nail in his mouth. The other three encircled him from below, with upturned faces and open mouths, like young birds expecting food. (Not that young birds expecting food wear gloves so appropriate to the occasion as were Emanuel's.) James Ollerenshaw was impressed by the workmanlike manner in which Andrew measured the width of the glass box and marked it off on the wall before beginning to knock nails. The presence of one nail in Andrew's mouth while he was knocking in the other with a coal hammer, prevented him from outraging the social code when the coal hammer embraced his fingers as well as the nail in the field of its activity. Unhappily, when it came to the second nail, no such hindrance operated.

The nails, having been knocked in, were duly and satisfactorily tested.

Then solemnly James seized the glass box containing the ship and ocean, and bore it with all possible precautions to the pair of steps in front of the great doors. Andrew descended two storeys, and, bending his body, received the box from James as a parson receives a baby at the font. He then remounted. The steps rocked.

'I'd happen better hold 'em,' said James.

'It'll be all right,' said Andrew.

'I'll hold them,' said Emanuel, hastening forward.

The precise cause of the accident will probably never be known, but no sooner did Emanuel lay his gloved hand on the steps than the whole edifice, consisting of steps, Andrew, and ship and ocean tottered and fell.

'Clumsy fool!' Andrew was distinctly heard to exclaim during his swift passage to the floor.

The ship and ocean were incurably disintegrated into a mess of coloured cardboard, linen, and sticks.

And catastrophes even more dreadful might have occurred had it not been for the calm and wise tact of Helen. Where a person is pleased by an event, that person can usually, without too much difficulty, exercise a calm and wise tact upon other persons whom the event has not pleased. And Helen was delighted by the catastrophe to the ship and ocean. The ship and ocean had formed no part in her scheme for the decoration of the hall; her one poor solace had been that the relative proportions of the hall and of the ship and ocean were such that even a careful observer might have spent hours in the former without discovering the latter; on the other hand some blundering ninny might have lighted instantly on the ship and ocean, and awkwardly inquired what it was doing there. So Helen was really enchanted by the ruin. She handled her men with notable finesse: Uncle James savage and vindictive, but uncertain upon whom to pour out his anger; Emanuel nursing his injured innocence; and Andrew Dean nursing his elbow, his head, and vengeance. She also found a moment in which to calm Georgiana, who had run flying and hysterical into the hall at the sound of the smash.

Even the steps were broken.

After a time harmony was established, both Uncle James and Emanuel being, at bottom, men of peace. But it was undeniable that Uncle James had lost more than gold, and that Emanuel had been touched in a perilous place – his conceit of himself.

Then Georgiana swept up the ship and ocean, and James retired to his own little room, where he assumed his Turkish cap, and began to arrange his personal effects in a manner definite and final, which would be a law for ever to the servants of Wilbraham Hall.

Left with the two young men, Helen went from triumph to triumph. In quite a few minutes she had them actually talking to each other. And she ended by speeding them away together. And by the time they departed each was convinced that Georgiana's apron, on Helen, was one of the most bewitching manifestations of the inexpressibly feminine that he had ever been privileged to see.

They took themselves off by a door at the farther end of the hall behind the stairs, whence there was a short cut through the undulating grounds to the main road.

Helen ascended to the state bedroom, where there was simply everything to be done; Georgiana followed her, after having made up the fires, and, while helping to unpack boxes, offered gossamer hints – fluffy, scarcely palpable, elusive things – to her mistress that her real ambition had always been to be a lady's-maid, and to be served at meals by the third, or possibly the fourth, house-maid. And the hall of Wilbraham Hall was abandoned for a space to silence and solitude.

Now, the window of Uncle James's little room was a little window that lived modestly between the double pillars of the portico and the first window of the great dining-room. Resting from his labours of sorting and placing, he gazed forth at his domain, and mechanically calculated what profit would accrue to him if he cut off a slip a hundred and fifty feet deep along by the Oldcastle Road, and sold it in lots for villas, or built villas and sold them on ninety-nine-year leases. He was engaged in his happy exercise of mental arithmetic when he heard footsteps crunching the gravel, and then a figure, which had evidently come round by the north side from the back of the Hall, passed across the field of James's vision. This figure was a walking baptism to the ground it trod. It dripped water plenteously. It was, in a word, soaked, and its garments clung to it. Its yellow chamois gloves clung to its hands. It had no hat. It hesitated in front of the entrance.

Uncle James pushed up his window. 'What's amiss, lad?' he inquired, with a certain blandness of satisfaction.

'I fell into the Water,' said Emanuel, feebly, meaning the sheet known as Wilbraham Water, which diversified the park-like splendours of Wilbraham Hall.

'How didst manage that?'

'The path is very muddy and slippery just there,' said Emanuel.

'Hadn't you better run home as quick as may be?' James suggested.

'I can't,' said Emanuel.

'Why not?'

'I've got no hat, and I'm all wet. And everybody in Oldcastle Road will see me. Can you lend me a hat and coat?'

And all the while he was steadily baptising the gravel.

Uncle James's head disappeared for a moment, and then he threw out of the window a stiff yellow mackintosh of great age. It was his rent-collecting mackintosh. It had the excellent quality of matching the chamois gloves.

Emanuel thankfully took it. 'And what about a cap or something?' he plaintively asked.

'Tak' this,' said Uncle James, with remarkable generosity whipping the Turkish cap from his own head and handing it to Emanuel.

Emanuel hesitated, then accepted; and, thus uniquely attired, sped away, still baptising.

At tea (tea proper) James recounted this episode to a somewhat taciturn and preoccupied Helen.

'He didn't fall into the Water,' said Helen, curtly. 'Andrew Dean pushed him in.'

'How dost know that?'

'Georgiana and I saw it from my bedroom window. It was she who first saw them fighting, or at any rate arguing. Then Andrew Dean "charged" him in, as if they were playing football, and walked on; and Emanuel Prockter scrambled out.'

'H'm!' reflected James. 'Well, if ye ask me, lass, Emanuel brought that on himsen. I never seed a man look a bigger foo' than Emanuel looked when he went off in my mackintosh and Turkish cap.'

'Your Turkish cap?'

'One of 'em.'

'With the tassel?'

'Ay!'

'It's a great shame! That's what it is! I'm sure he didn't look a fool! He's been very badly treated, and I'll —'

She rose from the table, in sudden and speechless indignation.

'You should ha' seen him, lass!' said James, and added: 'I wish ye had!' He tried to be calm. But she had sprung on him another of her disconcerting surprises. Was it, after all, possible, conceivable, that she was in love with Emanuel?

She sat down again. 'I know why you say that, uncle' – she looked him in the face, and put her elbows on the table. 'Now just listen to me!'

Highly perturbed, he wondered what was coming next.

CHAPTER XXII

CONFESSIONAL

'What's the matter with Emanuel Prockter?' Helen asked; meaning, what were the implied faults of Emanuel Prockter.

There was defiance in her tone. She had risen from the table, and she had sat down again, and she seemed by her pose to indicate that she had sat down again with a definite purpose, a purpose to do grievous harm to the soul's peace of anybody who differed from the statements which she was about to enunciate, or who gave the wrong sort of answers to her catechism. She was wearing her black mousseline dress (theoretically 'done with'), which in its younger days always had the effect of rousing the *grande dame* in her. She laid her ringless hands, lightly clasped, on a small, heavy, round mahogany table which stood in the middle of the little drawing-room, and she looked over James's shoulder into the vistas of the great drawing-room. The sombre, fading magnificence of the Wilbrahams – a magnificence of dark woods, tasselled curtains, reps, and gilt – was her theatre, and the theatre suited her mood.

Still, Jimmy Ollerenshaw, somewhat embittered by the catastrophe of the afternoon, conceived that he was not going to be browbeaten.

'What's the matter with Emanuel Prockter,' he said, 'is as he's probably gotten a cold by this.'

'Yes, and you're glad!' Helen retorted. 'You think he looked a fool after he'd been in the water. And you were glad.'

'I dunna' think,' said James, 'I'm sure.'

'But why should you be glad? That's what I want to know.'

James could not sagaciously reply to this query. He merely scratched his head, tilting one of his Turkish caps to that end.

'The fact is,' she cried, with a grammatical carelessness which was shocking in a woman who had professed to teach

120

everything, 'everyone has got their knives into Emanuel Prockter. And it's simply because he's good-looking and well-dressed and sings beautifully.'

'Good-looking!' murmured James.

'Well, isn't he?'

'He's pretty,' said James.

'No one ever said he had a lot of brains —'

'I never did,' James put in.

'But what does that matter? He *is* polite. He does know how to behave himself in polite society. If Andrew Dean pushed him into the water, that wasn't his fault. Andrew is stronger than he is, but that's no credit to Andrew Dean. It's to his discredit. Andrew Dean is nothing but a bully – we all know that. He might have pushed you into the water, or me.'

'He might,' James admitted, 'if I'd been silly enough to get between the water and him.'

'And I should like to know who looked a fool when Andrew Dean fell off those steps. And just listen to the language the man used. I will say this for Emanuel Prockter – I never heard him swear.'

'No,' said James. 'He wears gloves. He even wears 'em when he takes his bath of a November afternoon.'

'I don't care who knows it,' Helen observed, hotly. 'I like Emanuel Prockter.'

'There's nobody as dunna' know it,' said James. 'It's the talk of Bosley as you've set your cap at him.'

'I don't wear caps,' said Helen. 'I'm not a servant.'

'Hat, then,' James corrected himself. 'Ye'll not deny as you wear hats, I reckon. I've seen ye in forty.'

'I know who started that tale,' Helen exploded. 'Andrew Dean started that tale.'

'No,' said James. 'It was Mrs. Prockter, I'm thinking.'

'Has Mrs. Prockter spoken to you about me and – and Emanuel?'

James hesitated. But the devil-may-care, agreeably vicious Ollerenshaw impulses were afoot in him, and he did not hesitate long.

'Her has,' said he.

'What a ridiculous, fat old woman she is, with her fancies!'

Frankly, James did not like this. He was in a mind to resent

it, and then a certain instinct of self-preservation prompt-
ed him to seek cover in silence. But in any battle of the
sexes silence is no cover to the male, as he ought to have
known.

Helen pursued him behind his cover. 'I wonder who *she's*
setting her cap at! I suppose you'll not deny that *she* wears a
cap?'

It was quite a long time since James Ollerenshaw had
blushed; but he blushed at these words. Nothing could have
been more foolish, inept, on his part. Why should he blush
because Helen expressed a vague, hostile curiosity as to the
direction of Mrs. Prockter's cap? What had the direction of
Mrs. Prockter's cap to do with him? Yet blush he did. He
grew angry, not – curiously enough – with Helen, but with
himself and with Mrs. Prockter. His anger had the strange
effect of making him an arrant coward. He got up from his
chair, having pushed away his cup towards the centre of the
table. As tea was over he was within his rights in doing so.

'I mun be getting to work again,' he muttered.

'Please do wait a minute, uncle,' she said, imperiously.
'Can't you see I want to talk to you? Can't you see I've got
something on my mind?'

Deliberately challenged in this way, the formidable James
was no more than a sheep to the shearer. Until he met Helen,
he had perhaps never received deliberate, audacious chal-
lenges, and even now he was far from being accustomed to
them. So he just stood foolishly near his chair.

'I can't talk to you while you're standing up,' she said.

So he sat down. How simple it ought to have been for him
to exert authority over Helen, to tell her fiercely that he had no
intention of being talked to like that, and that if she persisted
in such tactics the front door was at her entire disposal! She
had no claim on him. Yet he ate his humble pie and sat down.

'So they are saying that there is something between Emanuel Prockter and me, are they?' she recommenced, in a new,
mollified voice, a voice that waved the white flag over her
head.

'It wouldna' surprise me to hear as they were,' said James.

'And supposing there *was* something between us, uncle,
should you mind?'

'I don't know as I should mind,' said he. 'And I don't know as it 'ud matter a brass button if I did mind.'

'What should you do, uncle?'

'I should do as I've always done,' said he; 'eat and sleep and take my walks abroad. Them as wants to marry will marry, and they will marry what suits 'em. But I shall tak' my meat and drink as usual.'

'Would you come to the wedding?'

'I've only got a funeral suit,' said he. 'But I'd buy me some togs if Emanuel 'ud tak' this place off my hands at what I gave.'

'Would you give me a wedding-present?'

'I'd give thee some advice. It's what thou'rt most in need of.'

His tone was gloomy and resigned.

She slipped round the table and sat on the arm of his chair.

'You are a horrid old thing,' she told him – not for the first time. 'I *am* in need of advice. And there's no one can give it me but you.'

'Nay, nay!' he recoiled. 'There's Sarah Swetnam. You're as thick as thieves.'

'She's the very last person I can go to,' said Helen.

'And why?'

'Why! Because Andrew is engaged to her sister, of course. That's the awful part of it.'

'Ay?' he questioned.

'Yes. Because, you see, it's Andrew Dean that I'm in love with.'

She said it in very pert and airy accents. And then the next moment she put James into terrible consternation by crying, and clutching his arm. He saw that she was serious. Light beat down upon him. He had to blink and collect himself.

'I' thy place, lass,' he said, 'I should keep that to mysen.'

'But I can't, uncle. That is, I haven't done. Andrew knows. You don't understand how much I'm in love with him. I've – he's —'

'Thou'st not kissed him?'

'Not exactly – but —'

'He's been kissing you in mistake for his other young woman?'

Helen nodded.

'Helen, what 'ud thy mother say?'

'It was because of Andrew Dean that I came to live in Bursley,' said she. 'I knew I shouldn't see him often enough if I stayed in Longshaw. So I came here. You know we had always liked each other, I *think*, ever since he spent two years at Longshaw at Spitz Brothers'. Then I didn't see him for some time. You know how rude and awkward he is. Well, there was a coolness. And then we didn't see each other for another long time. And when I next saw him I knew I really *was* in love with him. (Of course, I never said anything to mother. One doesn't, you know. And she was so taken up with her own affairs, poor dear!) And I thought he was really fond of me. I thought so because he was so cross and queer. He's like that, you know. And, after all, it was not that that made him cross and queer. It was just because he was as good as engaged to Lilian, and he didn't like to tell me. And I never knew. How could I guess? I'd never heard there was anything between him and Lilian. And besides, although he was cross and queer, he said things to me that he oughtn't to have said, considering how he was carrying on with Lilian. It was then that I settled on coming to Bursley. There was no *reason* why I should stay in Longshaw. I saw him again in Longshaw, *after* he was engaged to Lilian, and yet he never told me! And then, when I come here, the first thing I hear is that he's engaged to Lilian. It was that afternoon when Sarah called; do you remember, uncle?'

He remembered.

'I saw Mr. Dean that night, and somehow I told him what I thought of him. I don't know how it began; but I did. He said he couldn't help being engaged to Lilian. He said it was one of those engagements that go on by themselves, and you can't stop it. But he was engaged before he knew where he was – so he says. He said he preferred me, and if he'd known — So of course I was obliged to be very angry with him. That was why I didn't speak to him at first at Mrs. Prockter's; at least, that was partly why. The other reason was that he had accused me of running after Emanuel – of all people! I had been, you know. But what had that got to do with Andrew, seeing that he was engaged to Lilian? Besides, I'd been doing it on

purpose. And he was so *insolent*. And then, to crown all, Mrs.
Prockter makes me dance with him. No wonder I fainted! He
is the rudest, *rudest*, cruellest man I ever knew.'

She wiped her eyes.

'H'm!' mused James.

'He'll simply kill poor little Lilian!' She sobbed.

'What's that got to do with you, if you and Emanuel has got
nothing to do with him? It isn't you as'll be hung when
Lilian's murdered.'

'Can't you see he mustn't marry Lilian?' Helen burst out.
'Silly little thing! How can she understand him? She's miles
beneath him.'

'Is there anybody as does understand him?' James asked.

'I do,' she said. 'And that's flat. And I've got to marry him,
and you must help me. I wanted to tell you, and now I've told
you. Don't you think I've done right in being quite open with
you? Most girls are so foolish in these things. But I'm not.
Aren't you glad, uncle?'

'Glad inna' the word,' said he.

'*You must help me,*' she repeated.

CHAPTER XXIII

NOCTURNAL

Many things which previously had not been plain to James Ollerenshaw were plain to him that night, as, in the solitude of his chosen room he reflected upon the astonishing menu that Helen had offered him by way of supplement to his tea. But the chief matter in his mind was the great, central, burning, blinding fact of the endless worry caused to him by his connection with the chit. He had bought Wilbraham Hall under her threat to leave him if he did not buy it. Even at Trafalgar Road she had filled the little house with worry. And now, within a dozen hours of arising in it, she had filled Wilbraham Hall with worry – filled it to its farthest attic. If she had selected it as a residence, she would have filled the Vatican with worry. All that James demanded was a quiet life; and she would not let him have it. He wished he was back again in Trafalgar Road. He wished he had never met Helen and her sunshade in the park.

That is to say, he asserted to himself positively that he wished he had never met Helen. But he did not mean it.

And so he was to help her to wrest Andrew Dean from Lilian Swetnam! He was to take part in a shameful conspiracy! He was to assist in ruining an innocent child's happiness! And he was deliberately to foster the raw material of a scandal in which he himself would be involved! He, the strong, obstinate, self-centred old man who had never, till Helen's advent done anything except to suit his own convenience!

The one bright spot was that Helen had no genuine designs on Emanuel Prockter. As a son-in-law, Andrew Dean would be unbearable; but Emanuel Prockter would have been – well, impossible. Andrew Dean (he mused) was at any rate a man whom you could talk to and look at without feeling sick.

When he had gazed at the affair from all points of view, and repeated to himself the same deep moral truths (such as 'There's no doing nowt wi' a young woman afore she's forty'), about thirty-nine times, and pitied himself from every quarter of the compass, he rose to go to bed; he did not expect to sleep. But the gas was not yet in order, and he had only one candle, which was nearly at its latter end. The ladies – Helen and Georgiana – had retired long since.

He left his little room, and was just setting forth on the adventure of discovering his bedchamber, when a bell rang in the bowels of the house. His flesh crept. It was as if –

The clock struck twelve, and shook the silent tower.

Then he collected his powers of memory and of induction, and recognised in the sound of the bell the sound of the front door bell. Someone must be at the front door. The singular and highly-disturbing phenomena of distant clanging, of thrills, and of flesh-creepings were all resolved into the simple fact that someone was at the front door.

He went back into his little room; instead of opening the front door like a man, he opened the window of the little room, and stuck out the tassle of his cap.

'Who's there?' he demanded.

'It's I, Mr. Ollerenshaw,' said a voice, queenly and nervous.

'Not Mrs. Prockter?' he suggested.

'Yes.'

'I reckon ye'd like to come in,' he said.

She admitted the desire with a laugh which struck him as excessively free. He did not know whether to be glad or sorry that Helen had departed to bed. He did not even know whether to be glad or sorry that Mrs. Prockter had called. But he vividly remembered what Helen had said about caps.

Naturally, he had to let her in. He held the candle in his left hand, as he opened the door with his right, and the tassle of his cap was over his eye.

'You'll think I'm in the habit of calling on you at night,' said Mrs. Prockter, as she slid through the narrow space which James allotted to her, and she laughed again. 'Where is dear Helen?'

'She's gone to bed, missis,' said James, holding high the candle and gazing at the generous vision in front of him. It wore a bonnet, and a rich Paisley shawl over its flowered silk.

'But it's only ten o'clock!' Mrs. Prockter protested.

'Yes. But her's gone to bed.'

'Why,' Mrs. Prockter exclaimed, changing the subject wilfully, 'you are all straight here!' (For the carpets had been unrolled and laid.)

And she sat down on a massive Early Victorian mahogany chair about fifteen feet from the dying fire, and began to fan herself with her hands. She was one of your women who are never cold.

James, having nothing to say, said nothing, following his custom.

'I'm not ill-pleased,' said Mrs. Prockter, 'that Helen is out of the way. The fact is – it was you that I wanted to have a word with. You'll guess what about?'

'Mr. Emanuel?' James hazarded.

'Precisely. I had to put him to bed. He is certainly in for a very serious cold, and I trust – I fervently trust – it may not be bronchitis. That would mean nurses, and nothing upsets a house more than nurses. What happened Mr. Ollerenshaw?'

James set the candle down on another Early Victorian chair there being no occasional table at hand, and very slowly lowered himself to a sitting posture on a third.

'I'll tell you what happened, missis,' he said, putting his hands on his knees.

And he told her, beginning with the loss of the ship and ocean, and ending with Helen's ever memorable words: 'You must help me!'

'That's what happened, missis,' he said, grimly.

She had punctuated his recital by several exclamations, and when he had finished she gave rein to her sentiments.

'My *dear* Mr. Ollerenshaw,' she said, in the kindest manner conceivable, 'how I sympathise with you! How I wish I could help you!'

Her sympathy was a genuine comfort to him. He did not, in that instant, care a fig for Helen's notion about the direction of caps. He was simply and humanly eased by the sweet tones of this ample and comely dame. Besides, the idea of a woman such as Mrs. Prockter marrying a man such as him was (he knew) preposterous. She belonged to a little world which called him 'Jimmy,' whereas he belonged to a little world of his own. True, he was wealthy; but she was not poor – and no amount of money (he thought) could make a bridge to join those two worlds. Nevertheless, here she was, talking to him alone at ten o'clock at night – and not for the first time, either! Obviously, then, there was no nonsense about *her* whatever nonsensical world she belonged to.

She ran over with sympathy. Having no further fear of Helen making trouble in her own family, she had all her feelings at liberty to condone with James.

The candle, throwing a small hemisphere of feeble radiance in the vastness of the dim hall, sat on its chair between them.

'I *can* help you,' she said, suddenly, after grunts from James. 'I'm calling on the Swetnams the day after to-morrow. I'll tell them about – about to-day, and when Mrs. Swetnam asks me for an explanation of it, I will be mysterious. If Lilian is there, Mrs. Swetnam will certainly get her out of the room. Then I will just give the faintest hint that the explanation is merely jealousy between Emanuel and Mr. Dean concerning – a certain young lady. I shall treat it all as a joke; you can rely on me. Immediately I am gone Lilian will hear about it. She will quarrel with Andrew the next time she sees him; and if he *wishes* to be free, he may be.'

She smiled the arch, naughty, pleasantly-malign smile of a terribly experienced dowager. And she seemed positively anxious that James should have Andrew Dean for a son-in-law.

James, in his simplicity, was delighted. It appeared to him a Mephistophelian ingenuity. He thought how clever women were, on their own ground, and what an advantage they had in their immense lack of scruple.

'Of course,' said she, 'I have always said that a marriage between Andrew Dean and Lilian would be a mistake – a very serious mistake. They are quite unsuited to each other. She isn't in love with him – she's only been flattered by his attentions into drawing him on. I feel sorry for the little thing.'

At a stroke, she had converted a shameful conspiracy into an act of the highest virtue. And her smile changed, too –

became a *good* smile, a smile on which a man might depend. His heart went out to her, and he contemplated the smile in a pleased, beatific silence.

Just then the candle – a treacherous thing – flamed up and went out.

'Oh!' cried Mrs. Prockter.

And James had not a match. He never smoked. And without an atlas of the Hall, showing the location of match-boxes, he saw no hope of finding a match.

The fire was as good as one. A few cinders burnt red under the ash, showing the form of the chimney-piece, but no more.

'An ye got a match?' he asked her.

'No,' she said, drily, 'I don't carry matches. But I can tell you I don't like being in the dark at all.' Her voice came to him out of nothing, and had a most curious effect on his spine. Where are you, Mr. Ollerenshaw?'

'I'm a-sitting here,' he replied.

'Well,' said she, 'if *you* can't find a match, I think you had better lead me to the door. I certainly can't find my way there myself. Where is your hand?'

Then a hand touched his shoulder and burnt him. 'Is that you?' asked the voice.

'Ay!' he said.

And he took the hand, and the hand squeezed his hand – squeezed it violently. It may have been due to fear, it may have been due to mere inadvertence on the part of the hand; but the hand did, with unmistakable, charming violence, squeeze his hand.

And he rose.

'What's that light there?' questioned the voice, in a whisper.

'Where?' he whispered also.

'There – behind.'

He turned. A luminance seemed to come from above, from the unseen heights of the magnificent double staircase. As his eyes grew accustomed to the conditions, he gradually made out the details of the staircase.

'You'd better go and see,' the whispering voice comman-ded.

He dropped the hand and obeyed, creeping up the left wing of the staircase. As he faced about at the half-landing, he saw

Helen, in an orange-tinted peignoir, and her hair all down her back, holding a candle. She beckoned to him. He ascended to her.

'Who's there?' she inquired, coldly.

'Mrs. Prockter,' he murmured.

'And are you sitting together in the dark?' she inquired, coldly.

The story that the candle had expired seemed feeble in the extreme. And for him the word 'cap' was written in letters of fire on the darkness below.

He made no attempt to answer her question.

CHAPTER XXIV

SEEING A LADY HOME

Those words of Helen's began a fresh chapter in the life of her great-step-uncle, James Ollerenshaw. They set up in him a feeling, or rather a whole range of feelings, which he had never before experienced. At tea, Helen had hinted at the direction of Mrs. Prockter's cap. That was nothing. He could not be held responsible for the direction of Mrs. Prockter's cap. He could laugh at that, even though he faintly blushed. But to be caught sitting in the dark with Mrs. Prockter, after ten o'clock at night, in his own house; to have the fact pointed out to him in such a peculiar, meaningful tone as Helen employed – here was something that connected him and Mrs. Prockter in a manner just a shade too serious for mere smiling. Here was something that had not before happened to him in his career as rent-collector and sage.

Not that he minded! No, he did not mind. Although he had no intention whatever of disputing the possession of Mrs. Prockter with her stepson, he did not object to all the implication in Helen's remarkable tone. On the contrary, he was rather pleased. Why should not he sit with a lady in the dark? Was he not as capable as any man of sitting with a lady in the dark? He was even willing that Helen should credit him, or pretend to credit him, with having prearranged the dark.

Ah! People might say what they chose! But what a dog he might have been had he cared to be a dog! Here he was, without the slightest preliminary practice, successfully sitting with a lady in the dark, at the first attempt! And what lady? Not the first-comer! Not Mrs. Butt! Not the Mayoress! But the acknowledged Queen of Bursley, the undisputed leader of all that was most distinguished in Bursley society! And no difficulty about it either! And she had squeezed his hand. She had continued to squeeze it. She, in her rich raiment, with her

fine ways, and her correct accent, had squeezed the hand of
Jimmy Ollerenshaw, with his hard old clothes and his Turkish
cap, his simple barbarisms, his lack of style, and his uncom-
promising dialect! Why? Because he was rich? No. Because he
was a man, because he was the best man in Bursley, when you
came down to essentials.

So his thoughts ran.

His interest in Helen's heart had become quite a secondary
interest, but she recalled him to a sense of his responsibilities as
great-step-uncle of a capricious creature like her.

'What are you and Mrs. Prockter talking about?' she
questioned him in a whisper, holding the candle towards his
face and scrutinising it, as seemed to him, inimically.

'Well,' he said, 'if you must know, about you and that there
Andrew Dean.'

She made a brusque movement. And then she beckoned
him to follow her along the corridor, out of possible earshot of
Mrs. Prockter.

'Do you mean to say, uncle,' she demanded, putting the
candle down on a small table that stood under a large oil-
painting of Joshua and the Sun in the corridor, 'that you've
been discussing my affairs with Mrs. Prockter?'

He saw instantly that he had not been the sage he imagined
himself to be. But he was not going to be bullied by Helen, or
any other woman younger than Mrs. Prockter. So he stiffly
brazened it out.

'Ay!' he said.

'I never heard of such a thing!' she exploded, but still
whispering.

'You said as I must help ye, and I'm helping ye,' said he.

'But I didn't mean that you were to go chattering about me
all over Bursley, uncle,' she protested, adopting now the
pained, haughty, and over-polite attitude.

'I don't know as I've been chattering all over Bursley,' he
rebutted her. 'I don't know as I'm much of a chatterer. I might
name them as could give me a start and a beating when it
comes to talking the nose off a brass monkey. Mrs. Prockter
came in to inquire about what had happened here this afternoon, as well she might, seeing as Emanuel went home with a
couple o' gallons o' my water in his pockets. So I told her all

about it. Her's a very friendly woman. And her's promised to
do what her can for ye.'

'How?'

'Why, to get Andrew Dean for ye, seeing as ye're so fixed
on him, wi' as little gossip as maybe.'

'Oh! So Mrs. Prockter has kindly consented to get Andrew
Dean for me! And how does she mean to do it?'

James had no alternative; he was obliged to relate how Mrs.
Prockter meant to do it.

'Now, uncle,' said Helen, 'just listen to me. If Mrs.
Prockter says a single word about me to any one, I will never
speak either to her or you again. Mind! A single word! A nice
thing that she should go up to Swetnams's, and hint that
Andrew and Emanuel have been fighting because of me! What
about my reputation? And do you suppose that I want the
leavings of Lilian Swetnam? Me! The idea is preposterous!'

'You wanted 'em badly enough this afternoon,' said he.

'No, I didn't,' she contradicted him passionately. 'You are
quite mistaken. You misunderstood me, though I'm surprised
that you should have done. Perhaps I was a little excited this
afternoon. Certainly you were thinking about other things. I
expect you were expecting Mrs. Prockter this evening. It
would have been nicer of you to have told me she was
coming.'

'I —'

'Now, please let it be clearly understood,' she swept on.
'You must go down and tell Mrs. Prockter at once that you
were entirely in error, and that she is on no account to breathe
a word about me to any one. Whatever you were both
thinking of I cannot imagine! But I can assure you I'm
extremely annoyed. Mrs. Prockter putting her finger in the
pie! . . . Let her take care that I don't put my finger into *her*
pie! I always knew she was a gossiping old thing, but really —'

'Mr. Ollerenshaw!' A prettily plaintive voice rose from the
black depths below.

'There! she's getting impatient for you!' Helen snapped.
'Run off to her at once. To think that if I hadn't happened to
hear the bell ring, and come out to see what was the matter, I
should have been the talk of Bursley before I was a day older!'

She picked up the candle.

'I must have a light!' said James, somewhat lamely.

'Why?' Helen asked, calmly. 'If you could begin in the dark, why can't you finish in the dark? You and she seem to like being in the dark.'

'Mr. Ollerenshaw!' The voice was a little nearer.

'Her's coming!' James ejaculated.

Helen seemed to lose her courage before that threat.

'Here! Take this one, then!' said she, giving James her candle, and fleeing down the corridor.

James had the sensation of transacting a part in a play at a theatre where the scenery was absolutely realistic and at the same time of a romantic quality. Moonlight streaming in through the windows of the interminable corridor was alone wanting to render the illusion perfect. It was certainly astonishing – what you could buy with seven thousand two hundred and fifty pounds! Perhaps the most striking portion of the scenery was Helen's peignoir. He had not before witnessed her in a peignoir. The effect of it was agreeable; but, indeed, the modern taste for luxury was incredible! He wondered if Mrs. Prockter practised similar extravagances.

While such notions ran through his head he was hurrying to the stairs, and dropping a hail of candle-grease on the floor. He found Mrs. Prockter slowly and cautiously ascending the stairway. If he was at the summit of Mont Blanc, she had already reached Les Grands Mulets.

'What is it?' she asked, pausing, and looking up at him with an appealing gesture.

'What's what?'

'Why have you been so long?' It was as if she implied that these minutes without him were an eternity of ennui. He grew more and more conceited. He was already despising Don Juan as a puling boy.

'Helen heard summat, and so she had come out of her bedroom. Her's nervous i' this big house.'

'Did you tell her I was here, Mr. Ollerenshaw?'

By this time he had rejoined her at Les Grands Mulets.

'No,' he said, without sufficiently reflecting.

'She didn't hear me call out, then?'

'Did ye call out?' If he was in a theatre, he also could act.

'Perhaps it's just as well,' said Mrs. Prockter, after a

momentary meditation. 'Under the circumstances she cannot possibly suspect our little plot.'

Their little plot! In yielding to the impulse to tell her that Helen was unaware of her presence in the house he had forgotten that he had made it excessively difficult for him to demolish the said plot. He could not one moment agree with enthusiasm to the plot, and the next moment say that the plot had better be abandoned. Some men, doubtless, could. But he could not. He was scarcely that kind of man. His proper course would have been to relate to Mrs. Prockter exactly what had passed between himself and Helen, and trust to her commonsense. Unhappily, with the intention of pleasing her, or reassuring her, or something equally silly, he had lied to her and rendered the truth impracticable. However, he did not seem to care much. He had already pushed Helen's affairs back again to quite a secondary position.

'I suppose ye think it'll be all right, missis,' he said, carelessly – 'ye going up to Mrs. Swetnam's o' that 'n, and —'

'Rely on me,' said she, silencing him.

Thus, without a pang, he left Helen to her fate.

They had touched the ground-floor.

'Thank you very much, Mr. Ollerenshaw,' said Mrs. Prockter. 'Good-night. I'll make the best of my way home.'

Curious, how sorry he felt at this announcement! He had become quite accustomed to being a conspirator with her in the vast house lighted by a single candle, and he did not relish the end of the performance.

'I'll step along wi' ye,' said he.

'Oh, no!' she said. 'I really can't allow —'

'Allow what?'

'Allow you to inconvenience yourself like that for me.'

'Pooh!' said he.

And he, who had never in his life seen a lady to her door, set out on the business as though he had done nothing else every night of his life, as though it was an enterprise that did not require practice.

He opened the door, and put the candle on the floor behind it, where he could easily find it on returning. 'I'll get a box o' matches from somewhere while I'm out,' said he.

He was about to extinguish the candle when she stopped

him. 'Mr. Ollerenshaw,' she said, firmly, 'you haven't got your boots on. Those slippers are not thick enough for this weather.'

He gazed at her. Should he yield to her?

The idea of yielding to her, for the mere sake of yielding to her, presented itself to him as a charming idea. So he disappeared with the candle, and reappeared in his boots.

'You won't need a muffler?' she suggested.

Now was the moment to play the hardy Norseman. 'Oh, no!' he laughed.

This concern for his welfare, coming from such a royal creature, was, however, immensely agreeable.

She stood out on the steps; he extinguished the candle, and then joined her and banged the door. They started. Several hundred yards of winding pitch-dark drive had to be traversed.

'Will you kindly give me your arm?' she said.

She said it so primly, so correctly, and with such detachment, that they might have been in church, and she saying: 'Will you kindly let me look over your Prayer Book?'

When they arrived at the gas-lit Oldcastle Road he wanted to withdraw his arm, but he did not know how to begin withdrawing it.

Hence he was obliged to leave it where it was.

And as they were approaching the front gate of the residence of Mr. Buchanan, the Scotch editor of the *Signal*, a perfect string of people emerged from that front gate. Mrs. Buchanan had been giving a whist drive. There were sundry Swetnams among the string. And the whole string was merry and talkative. It was a fine night. The leading pearls of the string bore down on the middle-aged pair, and peered, and passed.

'Good-night, Mrs. Prockter. Good-night, Mr. Ollerenshaw.'

Then another couple did the same. 'Good-night, Mrs. Prockter. Good-night, Mr. Ollerenshaw.'

And so it went on. And the string, laughing and talking, gradually disappeared diminuendo in the distance towards Bursley.

'I suppose you know you've done it this time?' observed Mrs. Prockter.

It was a dark saying, but James fully understood it. He felt as though he had drunk champagne. 'As well be hung for a sheep as a lamb!' he said to himself. And deliberately squeezed the royal arm.

Nothing violent happened. He had rather expected the heavens to fall, or that at least Mrs. Prockter would exclaim: 'Unhand me, monster!' But nothing violent happened.

'And this is me, James Ollerenshaw!' he said to himself, still squeezing.

CHAPTER XXV

GIRLISH CONFIDENCES

One afternoon Sarah Swetnam called, and Helen in person opened the great door to the visitor.

'I saw that frock in Brunt's three days ago,' Helen began, kissing the tall, tight-bound, large-boned woman.

'I know you did, Nell,' Sarah admitted. 'But you needn't tell me so. Don't you like it?'

'I think it's a dream,' Helen replied, quickly. 'Turn round.' But there was a certain lack of conviction in her voice, and in Sarah's manner there was something strained. Accordingly, they both became extravagantly effusive – or, at any rate, more effusive than usual, though each was well aware that the artifice was entirely futile.

'All alone?' Sarah asked, when she had recovered from the first shock of the hall's magnificence.

'Yes,' said Helen. 'It's Georgiana's afternoon out, and uncle's away, and I haven't got any new servants yet.'

'Mr. Ollerenshaw away! No one ever heard of such a thing! If you knew him as well as we do, you'd have fainted with surprise. It ought to be in the paper. Where's he gone to?'

'He's gone to Derby, to try to buy some property that he says is going very cheap there. He's been gone three days now. He got a letter at breakfast, and said he must go to Derby at once. However, he had to finish his rents. The trouble is that his rents never are finished, and I'm bothered all the time by people coming with three and sixpence, or four shillings, and a dirty rent-book! Oh! and the dirt on the coins! My dear, you can't imagine! There's one good thing. He will have to come back for next week's rents. Not that I'm sorry he's gone. It gives me a chance, you see. By the time he returns I shall have my servants in.'

'Do tell me what servants you're going to have?'

'Well, I went to that agency at Oldcastle. I've got a German butler. He speaks four languages, and has beautiful eyes.'

'A German butler!'

If it had been a German prince Sarah could not have been more startled nor more delighted.

'Yes, and a cook, and two other maids; and a gardener and a boy. I shall keep Georgiana as my own maid.'

'My child, you're going it!'

'My child, I came here to go it.'

'And – and Mr. Ollerenshaw is really pleased?'

Helen laughed. 'Uncle never goes into raptures, you know. But I hope he will be pleased. The fact is, he doesn't know anything about these new servants yet. He'll find them installed when he returns. It will be a little treat for him. My piano came this morning. Care to try it?'

'Rather!' said Sarah. 'Well, I never saw anything like it!' This was in reference to her first glimpse of the great drawing-room. 'How you've improved it, you dear thing!'

'You see, I have my own cheque-book; it saves worry.'

'I see!' said Sarah, meaningly, putting her purse on the piano, her umbrella on a chair, and herself on the music-stool.

'Shall we have tea?' Helen suggested, after Sarah had performed on the Bechstein.

'Yes. Let me help you, do, dearest.'

They wandered off to the kitchens, and while they were seated at the kitchen-table, sipping tea, side by side, Sarah said:

'Now if you want an idea, I've got a really good one for you.'

'For me? What sort of an idea?'

'I'll tell you. You know Mrs. Wiltshire is dead.'

'I don't. I didn't even know there was a Mrs. Wiltshire.'

'Well, there was, and there isn't any longer. Mrs. Wiltshire was the main social prop of the old rector. And the annual concert of the St. Luke's Guild has always been held at her house, down at Shawport, you know. Awfully poky! But it was the custom since the Flood, and no one ever dared to hint at a change. Now the concert was to have been next week but one, and she's just gone and died, and the rector is wondering where he can hold it. I met him this morning. Why don't you let him hold it here? That would be a splendid way of opening your house – Hall, I beg its pardon. And you could introduce the beautiful eyes of your German butler to the entire neighbourhood. Of course, I don't know whether Mr. Ollerenshaw would like it.'

'Oh!' said Helen, without blenching, 'uncle would do as I wish.'

She mused, in silence, during a number of seconds.

'The idea doesn't appeal to you?' Sarah queried, disappointment in her tones.

'Yes, it does,' said Helen. 'But I must think it over. Now, would you care to see the rest of the house?'

'I should love to. Oh dear, I've left my handkerchief with my purse in the drawing-room.'

'Have mine!' said Helen, promptly.

But even after this final proof of intimate friendship, there still remained an obstinate trifle of insincerity in their relations that afternoon. Helen was sure that Sarah Swetnam had paid the call specially to say something, and that the something had not yet been said. And the apprehension of an impending scene gradually took possession of her nerves and disarranged them. When they reached the attics, and were enjoying the glorious views of the moorland in the distance and of Wilbraham Water in the immediate foreground, Helen said, very suddenly:

'Will the rector be in this afternoon?'

'I should say so. Why?'

'I was thinking we might walk down there together, and I could suggest to him at once about having the concert here.'

Sarah clapped her hands. 'Then you've decided?'

'Certainly.'

'How funny you are, Nell, with your decisions!'

In Helen's bedroom, amid her wardrobe, there was no chance of dangerous topics, the attention being monopolised by one subject, and that a safe one.

At last they went out together, two models of style and deportment, and Helen pulled to the great front door with a loud echoing clang.

'Fancy that place being all empty. Aren't you afraid of sleeping there while your uncle is away?'

'No,' said Helen. 'But I *should* be afraid if Georgiana wasn't afraid.'

After this example of courageous introspection, a silence fell upon the pair; the silence held firm while they got out of the grounds and crossed Oldcastle Road, and took to the Alls field-path, from which a unique panorama of Bursley – chimneys, kilns, canals, railways, and smoke-pall – is to be obtained. Helen was determined not to break the silence. And then came the moment when Sarah Swetnam could no longer suffer the silence; and she began, very cautiously:

'I suppose you've heard all about Andrew and Emanuel Prockter?'

Helen perceived that she had not been mistaken, and that the scene was at hand. 'No,' said she. 'What about them?'

'You don't mean to say you've not heard?'

'No. What about?'

'The quarrel between those two?'

'Emanuel and Mr. Dean?'

'Yes. But you must have heard?'

'I assure you, Sally, no one has told me a word about it.' (Which was just as true as it was untrue.)

'But they quarrelled up here. I *did* hear that Andrew threw Emanuel into your lake.'

'Who told you that?'

'It was Mrs. Prockter. She was calling on the mater yesterday, and she seemed to be full of it – according to the mater's account. Mrs. Prockter's idea was that they had quarrelled about a woman.'

('Mrs. Prockter shall be repaid for this,' said Helen to herself.)

'Surely Emanuel hasn't been falling in love with Lilian, has he?' said Helen, aloud. She considered this rather clever on her part. And it was.

'Oh, no!' replied Sally, positively. 'It's not Lilian.' And there was that in her tone which could not be expressed in ten volumes. 'You know perfectly well who the woman is,' Helen seemed to hear her say.

Then Helen said: 'I think I can explain it. They were both at our house the day we removed.'

'Oh, *were* they?' murmured Sarah, in well-acted surprise.

'And Mr. Dean fell off some steps that Emanuel was supposed to be holding. I *thought* he was furious – but not to that point. That's probably the secret of the whole thing. As for Mr. Dean having pushed Emanuel into the lake, I don't believe a word of it.'

'Then how was it that Emanuel had a cold and had to stay in bed?'

'My dear, to have a cold it isn't necessary to have been thrown into Wilbraham Water!'

'That's true,' Sarah admitted.

'However,' Helen calmly proceeded, 'I'll find out all about it and let you know.'

'How shall you find out?'

'I shall make Emanuel tell me. He will tell me anything. And he's a dear boy.'

'Do you see him often up here?' Sarah inquired.

'Oh, yes!' This was not true. 'We get on together excellently. And I'm pretty sure that Emanuel is not – well – interested in any other woman. That's why I should say that they have not been quarrelling about a woman. Unless, of course, the woman is myself.' She laughed, and added: 'But I'm not jealous. I can trust Emanuel.'

And with marvellous intrepidity she looked Sarah Swetnam in the face.

'Then,' Sarah stammered, 'You and Emanuel – you don't mean —'

'My dear Sally, don't you think Emanuel is a perfectly delightful boy?'

'Oh, *yes!*' said Sarah.

'So do I,' said Helen.

'But are you —'

'Between ourselves,' Helen murmured. 'Mind you, between our*selves* – I could imagine stranger things happening.'

'Well,' said Sarah, 'this *is* news.'

'Mind, not a syllable!'

'Oh, of course not.'

'By the way,' Helen asked, 'when are Andrew and Lilian going to get married?'

'I don't know. No one knows. One confidence for another, my dear; they don't always hit it off.'

'What a pity!' Helen remarked. 'Because if ever two people were suited to each other in this world, they are. But I hope they'll shake down.'

They arrived at the rector's.

CHAPTER XXVI

THE CONCERT

On another afternoon a middle-aged man and a young-hearted woman emerged together from Bursley Railway Station. They had a little luggage, and a cab from the Tiger met them by appointment. Impossible to deny that the young-hearted one was wearing a flowered silk under a travelling mantle. The man, before getting into the cab, inquired as to the cost of the cab. The gold angel of the Town Hall rose majestically in front of him, and immediately behind him the Park, with the bowling-green at the top, climbed the Moorthorne slope. The bowling season was of course over, but even during the season he had scarcely played. He was a changed person. And the greatest change of all had occurred that very morning. Throughout a long and active career he had worn paper collars. Paper collars had sufficed him, and they had not shocked his friends. But now he wore a linen collar, and eleven other linen collars were in his carpet-bag. Yet it has been said, by some individual who obviously lacked experience of human nature, that a man never changes the style of his collar after forty.

The cab drove up to Hillport, and deposited flowered silk and one bag at the residence of Mrs. Prockter. It then ascended higher, passing into the grounds of Wilbraham Hall, and ultimately stopping at the grandiose portals thereof, which were wide open.

The occupant of the cab was surprised to see two other cabs just departing. The next moment he was more than surprised – he was startled. A gentleman in evening dress stood at the welcoming doors, and on perceiving him this gentleman ran down the steps, and, with a sort of hurried grace, took his carpet-bag from him, addressing him in broken English, and indicating by incomprehensible words and comprehensible signs that he regarded him, the new arrival, as the light of his eyes and the protector of the poor and of the oppressed. And no sooner had he got the new arrival safe into the hall than he stripped him of hat, coat, and muffler, and might have proceeded to extremes had not his attention been distracted by another vehicle.

This vehicle contained the aged rector of Bursley.

'Ha! Mr. Ollerenshaw!' cried the divine. 'Your niece told me only yesterday that you were still in Derby buying property, and would not be back.'

'I've bought it, parson,' said James.

'Ha! ha!' said the divine, rubbing his hands. He stooped habitually, which gave him the air of always trying to glimpse at his toes over the promontory of his waist. And as James made no reply to the remark, he repeated: 'Ha! ha! So you decided to come to my concert, eh?'

'I only heard of it yesterday,' said James.

'Well,' said the divine, 'I'm afraid they'll be waiting for me. Ha! ha! This way, isn't it? Fine place you've got here. Very fine! Noble!'

And he disappeared through the double doors that led to the drawing-room, which doors were parted for him by a man-ikin whose clothes seemed to be held together by new sixpences. During the brief instant of opening, a vivacious murmur of conversation escaped like gas from the drawing-room into the hall.

James glanced about for his bag – it was gone. The gentleman in evening dress was out on the steps. Disheartened by the mysterious annihilation of his old friend the bag, James, weary with too much and too various emotion, went slowly up the grand staircase. In his bedroom the first thing he saw was his bag, which had been opened and its contents suitably bestowed. Thus his hair-brushes were on the dressing-table. This miracle completed his undoing. He sat down on an easy-chair, drew the eider-down off the bed, and put it on his knees, for the temperature was low. He did not intend to go to sleep. But he did go to sleep. It was simply a case of nature recovering from emotions.

He slept about an hour, and then, having brushed his wispish hair, he descended the stairs, determined to do or die.

Perhaps he would not have plumped himself straight into the drawing-room had not the manikin clad in sixpences assumed that the drawing-room was his Mecca and thrown open the doors.

A loud 'Hush!' greeted him. The splendid chamber was full of women's hats and men's heads; but hats predominated. And the majority of the audience were seated on gilt chairs which James had never before seen. Probably there were four or five score gilt chairs. At the other end of the room the aged rector sat in an easy-chair. Helen herself was perched at the piano, and in front of the piano stood Emanuel Prockter. Except that the room was much larger, and that, instead of faultless evening dress, Emanuel wore a faultless frock-coat (with the rest of a suit), the scene reminded James of a similar one on the great concertina night at Mrs. Prockter's.

Many things had happened since then. Still, history repeats itself.

'O Love!' exclaimed Emanuel Prockter, adagio and soste-nuto, thus diverting from James a hundred glances which James certainly was delighted to lose.

And Helen made the piano say 'O Love!' in its fashion.

And presently Emanuel was launched upon the sea of his yearnings, and voyaging behind the hurricane of passion. And, as usual, he hid nothing from his hearers. Then he hove to, and, as it were, climbed to the main-topgallant-sail in order to announce:

'O Love!'

It was not surprising that his voice cracked. Emanuel ought to have been the last person to be surprised at such a phenomenon. But he was surprised. To him the phenomenon of that cracking was sempiternally novel and astounding. It pained and shocked him. He wondered whose the fault could be? And then, according to his habit, he thought of the pianist. Of course, it was the fault of the pianist. And, while conti-nuing to sing he slowly turned and gazed with sternness at the pianist. The audience must not be allowed to be under any misapprehension as to the identity of the culprit. Unfortun-ately, Emanuel, wrapped up, like the artist he was, in his performance, had himself forgotten the identity of the culprit. Helen had ceased to be Helen; she was merely his pianist. The

thing that he least expected to encounter when gazing sternly
at the pianist was the pianist's gaze. He was accustomed to
flash his anger on the pianist's back. But Helen, who had seen
other pianists at work for Emanuel, turned as he turned, and
their eyes met. The collision disorganised Emanuel. He continued to glare with sternness, and he ceased to sing. A
contretemps had happened. For the fifth of a second everybody felt exceedingly awkward. Then Helen said, with a faint
cold smile, in a voice very low and very clear:

'What's the matter with you, Mr. Prockter? It wasn't my
voice that cracked.'

The minx!

There was a half-hearted attempt at the maintenance of the
proprieties, and then Wilbraham Hall rang with the laughter
of a joke which the next day had become the common
precious property of all the Five Towns. When the aged rector
had restored his flock to a sense of decency Mr. Emanuel
Prockter had vanished. In that laughter his career as a singer
reached an abrupt and final conclusion. The concert also came
to an end. And the collection, by which the divine always
terminated these proceedings, was the largest in the history of
the Guild.

A quarter of an hour or twenty minutes later all the guests,
members, and patrons of the St. Luke's Guild had left, most of
them full of kind inquiries after Mr. Ollerenshaw, the genial
host of that so remarkably successful entertainment. The
appearances and disappearances of Mr. Ollerenshaw had been
a little disturbing. First it had been announced that he was
detained in Derby, buying property. Indeed, few persons
were unaware that, except for a flying visit in the middle, of
two days, to collect his rents, James had spent a fortnight in
Derby purchasing sundry portions of Derby. Certainly Helen
had not expected him. Nor had she expected Mrs. Prockter,
who two days previously had been called away by telegram to
the bedside of a sick cousin in Nottingham. Nor had she
expected Lilian Swetnam, who was indisposed. The unexpected ladies had not arrived; but James had arrived, as disconcerting as a ghost, and then had faded away with equal
strangeness. None of the departing audience had seen even the
tassel of his cap.

Helen discovered him in his little room at the end of the hall. She was resplendent in black and silver.

'So here you are, uncle!' said she, and kissed him. 'I'm so glad you got back in time. Can you lend me sixpence?'

'What for, lass?'

'I want to give it to the man who's taking away the chairs I had to hire.'

'What's become o' that seven hundred and seventy pound odd, as ye had?'

'Oh,' she said, lightly, 'I've spent that.' She thought she might as well have done with it, and added: 'And I'm in debt – lots. But we'll talk about that later. Sixpence, please.'

He blenched. But he, too, had been expensive in the pursuit of delight. He, too, had tiresome trifles on his mind. So he produced the sixpence, and accepted the dissipation of nearly eight hundred pounds in less than a month with superb silence.

Helen rang the bell. 'You see, I've had all the bells put in order,' she said.

The gentleman in evening dress entered.

'Fritz,' said she, 'give this sixpence to the man with the chairs.'

'Yes, miss,' Fritz dolefully replied. 'A note for you, miss.'

And he stretched forth a charger on which was a white envelope.

'Excuse me, uncle,' said she, tearing the envelope.

'Dinna' mind me, lass,' said he.

The note ran:

'I must see you by the Water to-night at nine o'clock. Don't fail, or there will be a row. – A.D.'

She crushed it.

'No answer, Fritz,' said she. 'Tell cook, dinner for two.'

'Who's he?' demanded James, when Fritz had bowed himself out.

'That's our butler,' said Helen, kindly. 'Don't you like his eyes?'

'I wouldna' swop him eyes,' said James. He could not trust himself to discuss the butler's eyes at length.

'Don't be late for dinner, will you, uncle?' she entreated him.

'Dinner!' he cried. 'I had my dinner at Derby. What about my tea?'

'I mean tea,' she said.

He went upstairs again to his room, but he did not stay there a moment. In the corridor he met Helen, swishing along.

'Look here, lass,' he stopped her. 'A straight question deserves a straight answer. I'm not given to curiosity as a rule, but what is Emanuel Prockter doing on my bed?'

'Emanuel Prockter on your bed!' Helen repeated, blankly. He saw that she was suffering from genuine surprise.

'On my bed!' he insisted.

The butler appeared, having heard the inquiry from below. He explained that Mr. Prockter, after the song, had come to him and asked where he could lie down, as he was conscious of a tendency to faint. The butler had indicated Mr. Ollerenshaw's room as the only masculine room available.

'Go and ask him how he feels,' Helen commanded.

Fritz obeyed, and returned with the message that Mr. Prockter had 'one of his attacks,' and desired his mother.

'But he can't have his mother,' said Helen. 'She's at Nottingham. He told me so himself. He must be delirious.' And she laughed.

'No, her isn't,' James put in. 'Her's at wum' (home).

'How do you know, uncle?'

'I know,' said James. 'Her'd better be sent for.'

And she was sent for.

CHAPTER XXVII

UNKNOTTING AND KNOTTING

When Mrs. Prockter arrived it was obvious to Helen, in spite of her wonderful calm upon discovering James Ollerenshaw's butler and page, that the lady was extremely ill-at-ease. And Helen, though preoccupied herself by matters of the highest personal importance, did what she could to remedy a state of affairs so unusual. Probably nobody, within the memory of that generation, had ever seen Mrs. Prockter ill-at-ease. Helen inquired as to the health of the sick relative at Nottingham, and received a reply in which vagueness was mingled with hesitancy and a blush. It then became further obvious to the perspicuous Helen that Mrs. Prockter must have heard of her stepsons's singular adventure, and either resented Helen's share in it, or was ashamed of Emanuel's share in it.

'You know that Emanuel is here?' said Helen, with her most diplomatic and captivating smile.

But Mrs. Prockter did not know. 'I thought Mr. Ollerenshaw wanted me,' Mrs. Prockter explained, 'so I came as quickly as I could.'

'It was I who wanted to speak to you,' said Helen. 'The truth is that Emanuel is lying on uncle's bed, unwell or something, and he expressed a wish to see you. He was singing at the concert —'

'So sorry I wasn't able to be here,' Mrs. Prockter inserted, with effusive anxiety.

'We missed you awfully,' Helen properly responded. 'The rector was inconsolable. So was everybody,' she added feeling that as a compliment the rector's grief might be deemed insufficient. 'And he had a break-down.'

'Who? Emanuel?'

'Yes. I was accompanying him, and I am afraid it was my fault. Anyhow, he didn't finish his song. And then we missed

151

him. He had asked the butler to let him lie down somewhere, and uncle found him in his bedroom. I hope it's nothing serious.'

'Oh, my dear girl,' said Mrs. Prockter, regaining somewhat her natural demeanour in a laugh, 'if it's only one of Emanuel's singing breakdowns, we needn't worry. Can I go up and talk sense to him? He's just like a child, you know.'

'Let me take you up,' cried Helen.

And the two women ascended the grand staircase. It was the first time the grand staircase had been used with becoming dignity since Mrs. Prockter had used it on her visit of inspection. That staircase and Mrs. Prockter were made for each other.

No sooner had they disappeared than James popped out of his lair, where he had been hiding, and gazed up the staircase like a hunter stalking his prey. The arrival of the page in sixpences put him out of countenance for a moment, especially when the page began to feed the hall-fire in a manner contrary to all James's lifelong notions of feeding fires. However, he passed the time by giving the page a lesson.

Helen tapped at the bedroom door, left Mrs. Prockter to enter, and descended the stairs again.

'Is her up there with him?' James asked, in a whisper.

Helen nodded.

'Ye'd better ask her stop and have something to eat wi' us,' said James.

Helen had to reconcile James Ollerenshaw to the new scale of existence at Wilbraham Hall. She had to make him swallow the butler, and the page, and the other servants, and the grand piano – in themselves a heavy repast – without counting the evening dinner. Up to the present he had said nothing, because there had been no fair opportunity to say anything. But he might start at any moment. And Helen had no reason to believe that he had even begun the process of swallowing. She argued, with a sure feminine instinct and a large experience of mankind, that if he could only be dodged into tacitly accepting the new scale for even a single meal, her task would be very much simplified. And what an ally Mrs. Prockter would be!

'Tell cook there will be three to dinner,' she said to the page, who fled gleefully.

After a protracted interval Mrs. Prockter reappeared. 'She began by sighing. 'The foolish boy is seriously damaged,' said she.

'Not hurt?' Helen asked.

'Yes. But only in his dignity. He pretends it's his throat, but it isn't. It's only his dignity. I suppose all singers are children, like that. I'm really ashamed to have to ask you to let him lie there a little, dear Miss Rathbone; but he is positively sure that he can't get up. I've been through these crises with him before, but never one quite so bad.'

She laughed. They all laughed.

'I'll let him lie there on one condition,' Helen sweetly replied. 'And that is that you stay to dinner. I am relying on you. And I won't take a refusal.'

Mrs. Prockter looked sharply at James, and James blushed.

'James,' she exclaimed, 'you've told her. And you promised you wouldn't till tomorrow.'

'Nay!' said James. 'I've said nowt! It's you as has let it out, *now*, missis!'

'Told me what, Mrs. Prockter?' Helen asked, utterly unexpectant of the answer she was to get.

'My dear girl,' said the elder dame, 'do not call me Mrs. Prockter. I am Mrs. Ollerenshaw. I am the property that your uncle has been buying at Derby. And he is my sick relative at Nottingham. We preferred to do it like that. We could not have survived engagements and felicitations.'

'Oh, you wicked sinners! You – you terrible darlings!' Helen burst out as soon as she could control her voice.

Mrs. Ollerenshaw wept discreetly.

'Bless us! Bless us!' murmured James not to beseech a benediction, but simply to give the impression (quite false) that, in his opinion, much fuss was being made about nothing.

The new scale of existence was definitely accepted. And in private Mrs. Ollerenshaw entirely agreed with Helen as to the merits of the butler.

After dinner James hurried to his lair to search for a book. The book was not where he had left it, on his original entry into Wilbraham Hall. Within two minutes, the majority of the household staff was engaged in finding that book. Ultimately the butler discovered it; the butler had been reading it.

'Ay!' said James, opening the volume as he stood in front of the rich, expensive fire in the hall. 'Dickens – Charles Dickens – that's the chap's name. I couldn't think of it when I was telling you about th' book th' other day. I mun' go on wi' that.'

'Couldn't you play us something?' responded his wife.

In the triumph of concertinas over grand pianos, poor Emanuel, lying wounded upstairs, was forgotten. At five minutes to nine Helen stole, unperceived, away from the domestic tableau. She had by no means recovered from her amazement; but she had screened it off by main force in her mind, and she was now occupied with something far more important than the blameless amours of the richest old man in Hillport.

By Wilbraham Water a young man was walking to and fro in the deep autumn night. He wore a cap and a muffler, but no overcoat, and his hands were pushed far down into the pockets of his trousers. He regarded the ground fixedly, and stamped his feet at every step. Then a pale grey figure, with head enveloped in a shawl, and skirts carefully withdrawn from the ground, approached him.

He did not salute the figure, he did not even take his hands out of his pockets. He put his face close to hers, and each could see that the other's features were white and anxious.

'So you've come,' said he, glumly.

'What do you want?' Helen coldly asked.

'I want to speak to you. That's what I want. If you care for Emanuel Prockter, why did you play that trick on him this afternoon?'

'What trick?'

'You know perfectly well what I mean. So I'll thank you not to beat about the bush. The plain fact is that you don't care a pin for Prockter.'

'I never said I did.'

'You've made everyone believe you did anyhow. You've even made me think so, though all the time I knew it was impossible. An ass like that!'

'What do you want?' Helen repeated.

They were both using a tone intended to indicate that they were enemies from everlasting to everlasting, and that mere words could not express the intensity of their mutual hatred and scorn. The casual distant observer might have conceived the encounter to be a love idyll.

There was a short silence.

'I broke off my engagement last night,' Andrew Dean muttered, ferociously.

'Really!' Helen commented.

'You don't seem to care.'

'I don't see what it has to do with me. But if you talked to Lilian Swetnam in the same nice agreeable manner that you talk to me, I can't say I'm surprised to hear that she broke with you.'

'Who told you *she* broke?' Andrew demanded.

'I guessed,' said Helen. 'You'd never have had the courage to break it off yourself.'

Andrew made a vicious movement.

'If you mean to serve me as you served Emanuel,' she remarked, with bitter calm, 'please do it as gently as you can. And don't throw me far. I can only swim a little.'

Andrew walked away.

'Good-night,' she called.

'Look here!' he snarled, coming back to her. 'What's the matter with you? I know I oughtn't to have asked Lilian to marry me. Everybody knows that. It's universally agreed. But are you going to make that an excuse for spoiling the whole show? What's up with you is pride.'

'And what is up with you?' she inquired.

'Pride,' said he. 'How could I know you were in love with me all the time? How could —'

'You couldn't,' said Helen. 'I wasn't. No more than you were with me.'

'If you weren't in love with me, why did you try to make me jealous?'

'Me try to make you jealous!' she exclaimed, disdainfully. 'You flatter yourself Mr. Dean!'

'I can stand a good deal, but I can't stand lies, and I won't!' he exploded. 'I say you did try to make me jealous.'

He then noticed that she was crying.

The duologue might have extended itself indefinitely if her tears had not excited him to uncontrollable fury, to that instinctive cruelty that every male is capable of under certain conditions. Without asking her permission, without uttering a word of warning, he rushed at her and seized her in his arms. He crushed her with the whole of his very considerable strength. And he added insult to injury by kissing her about forty-seven times. Women are such strange, incalculable creatures. Helen did not protest. She did not invoke the protection of Heaven. She existed, passively and silently, the unremonstrating victim of his disgraceful violence.

Then he held her at arm's length. 'Will you marry me?'

'Yes,' she said.

'Did you try to make me jealous?'

'Yes.'

Later, as they walked by the lake, he ejaculated; 'I'm an awful brute!'

'I like you as you are,' she replied.

But the answer was lacking in precision, for at that moment he was being as tender as only an awful brute can be.

'Of course,' she said, 'we mustn't say anything about it yet.'

'No,' he agreed. 'To let it out at once might make unpleasantness between you and the Swetnams.'

'Oh!' she said, 'I wasn't thinking of that. But there's another love-affair in the house, and no house will hold two at once. It would be nauseating.'

That is how they talk in the Five Towns. As if one could have too much love, even in a cottage – to say nothing of a Wilbraham Hall! Mrs. Ollerenshaw placidly decided that she and James would live at the Hall, though James would have preferred something a size smaller. As I have already noticed, the staircase suited her; James suited her too. No one could guess why, except possibly James. They got on together, as the Five Towns said, 'like a house afire.'

Helen and Andrew Dean were satisfied with a semi-detached villa in Park Road, with a fine view of the gold angel. Women vary, capricious beings! Helen is perfectly satisfied with one servant. But she dresses rather better than ever.

THE END

WILKIE COLLINS

THE BITER BIT
& OTHER STORIES

Here are tales of detection, mystery and suspense, from the author of *The Moonstone* and *The Woman in White*.

The title story is an investigation into an unusual robbery, revealing Wilkie Collins' little known comic talents. Others selected for inclusion are *A Terribly Strange Bed*, set in a Parisian gambling den, where a young Englishman encounters the 'fiendish murder machine' after breaking the bank; *Mad Monkton*, a fine thriller; *Gabriel's Marriage*, set at the time of the French Revolution and an intriguing mystery, *The Lady of Glenwith Grange*.

DANIEL DEFOE

CAPTAIN SINGLETON

Defoe had that power to create the illusion of truth which is the very life force of fiction and nowhere is this more evident than in his portrait of the piratical Captain Singleton.

Taken by a gypsy child-stealer, Singleton soon finds himself cast ashore on the island of Madagascar. How he crosses Africa with a party of marooned sailors from Mozambique to the Gold Coast is a book in itself. His years of piracy are still to come. The story moves to the West Indies where he falls in with William the Quaker, an unusual pirate with whom Singleton becomes a lifelong friend, sharing adventures from the Spanish Main to the Indian Ocean before, filled with remorse, he decides to end it all . . .

ARTHUR
CONAN DOYLE

THE LOST WORLD

The Lost World is the story of an expedition by four men to a remote plateau in South America, a region out of time, cut off from the outside world by unscaleable, vertical cliffs. In an area the size of an English county, pterodactyls, iguanodons, ape men and dinosaurs still exist.

Into this nightmare world come Professor Challenger, Summerbee, Lord John Roxton and the reporter Malone. After many adventures they return at last to London with proof of their incredible discovery.

Conan Doyle tried in vain to kill off his more famous creation, Sherlock Holmes, but in the character of Challenger, he was content.

THOMAS HARDY

A GROUP OF NOBLE DAMES

The ten stories contained in *A Group of Noble Dames* are ranged around a '. . . store of ladies, whose bright eyes rain influence'.

Hardy plumbs the hidden depths of county families to reveal what went on behind the scenes, transforming half-remembered incidents into palpitating drama. Barbara of the House of Grebe, Lady Mottisfont, Anna, Lady Baxby, The Lady Penelope and The Honourable Laura, together with the other Noble Dames, will live long in the mind of the reader.

THOMAS HARDY
LIFE'S LITTLE IRONIES

Hardy considered 'The Son's Veto' to be his best short story, whilst 'On The Western Circuit' was Florence Hardy's favourite. It is difficult to argue with either judgement, for each of the tales in *Life's Little Ironies* will be championed by different readers. Suffice to say that they show Hardy at his characteristic best in the Wessex countryside he made his own.

As a pendant to the tales, Hardy added a series of stories linked under the heading 'A Few Crusted Characters', harking back to an earlier age. The characters are here in good measure – Tony Kytes, Andrey Satchel and the rest – their stories told to a returning native by Burthen, the Longpuddle Carrier, during a golden afternoon in autumn.

ANTHONY TROLLOPE

THE SPOTTED DOG & OTHER STORIES

Here is a fine assortment, as good as anything that came from Trollope's pen. These stories are presented as the collection of London magazine editors, gleaned over the years in their search for new material for their readers; tales of sorrow and mirth, suffering and delight.

The title story takes the reader into the dark world of Victorian London, with its squalid back streets surrounding The Spotted Dog public house. In the five remaining tales, a stream of characters is given life by the author, each with a story to tell as fascinating and diverse as anything likely to pass through an editor's hands. All are guaranteed to delight the reader.

ANTHONY TROLLOPE

THE VICAR OF BULLHAMPTON

Here is another of Trollope's splendid galleries of characters: Harry Gilmore, the Squire, Captain Walter Marrable, the Reverend Frank Fenwick and Mrs. Fenwick, who is as good a specimen of an English country parson's wife as you shall meet in any county – good-looking, fond of the society around her, with a little dash of fun, knowing in blankets and corduroys and coals and tea – knowing also in beer and gin and tobacco.

Between them, the Vicar of Bullhampton and his wife are acquainted with every man and woman in the parish, including the Balfours, Mary Lowther and the Brattles – the Brattles who live across the meadows at the old mill and who are to figure so prominently in this story, set in a quiet Wiltshire backwater.